# Murder on the Ballot

**A Myrtle Clover Cozy Mystery, Volume 17**

Elizabeth Spann Craig

Published by Elizabeth Spann Craig, 2020.

This is a work of fiction. Similarities to real people, places, or events are entirely coincidental.

MURDER ON THE BALLOT

**First edition. December 1, 2020.**

Copyright © 2020 Elizabeth Spann Craig.

Written by Elizabeth Spann Craig.

# Chapter One

"Are you done with the comics?" asked Miles as Myrtle frowned ferociously at the first section of the newspaper.

"Hmm?"

"The comics. I need something to wake me up a little," said Miles. He looked at the clock on Myrtle's wall and groaned. "It's not fair that I'm drowsy now. I couldn't have been drowsy at four a.m.?"

Myrtle said, "Well, the pancakes you made probably didn't help, although they were very good."

"I thought carbs were supposed to give us energy."

"I think it's supposed to be the kind of temporary energy that we crash from, later on," said Myrtle. She tossed the newspaper down with a disgusted sigh.

"I guess you're done with *that* section of the paper, at any rate," said Miles.

Myrtle said, "I think what I'm done with is the complete and total foolishness that's evident on our town council. They can't really seem to get anything accomplished and it's most vexing. They squabble constantly."

"Perhaps you should run for office," said Miles mildly as Myrtle thrust the comics section at him.

Myrtle paused, staring at him. "Why not?"

Miles glanced up from reading Peanuts, wrinkling his forehead in confusion. "What?"

"Oh, pay attention, Miles! You just offered me a very valuable suggestion you know." Pasha, Myrtle's feral cat, jumped up on her lap and Myrtle rubbed her. She crooned, "What a good girl, Pasha. See, Pasha thinks it's a good idea, too. You have these moments of brilliance, you know."

Miles was still trying to work out exactly what his brilliant moment had been. He remembered asking for the comics section. He'd made pancakes. There'd been some talk about carbs. Then he remembered.

"You aren't serious, Myrtle."

"Why not? Why *shouldn't* I run for office?"

Miles said, "It will probably make your blood pressure rise to unacceptable levels."

"My blood pressure is always ninety over sixty," said Myrtle proudly.

Miles gaped at her. "Isn't that very low?"

"*Admirably* low."

"Not *too* low? Don't you see dots and fuzzy things if you stand up too quickly?"

Myrtle said, "Not one bit. I'm not on any medication whatsoever for it, unlike my son. Red, as you know, has a terrible blood pressure problem."

Myrtle said the last bit rather smugly. Red was her son, in his late forties. He was police chief of the small town of

# MURDER ON THE BALLOT

Bradley, North Carolina, where they lived. Miles strongly suspected, however, that it wasn't the job that made Red have a blood pressure problem, but his octogenarian mother and her capers.

This belief was once again supported when Myrtle said gleefully, "Think how exasperated Red will be over it."

"Is there even an open seat on the council?" asked Miles.

"There sure is. Damian Cooper dropped dead at dinner just last month, remember? They'll be having to replace him on the council." Myrtle's tone, when speaking of Damian Cooper, was rather too cheerful.

Miles said slowly, "But the council is a lot of work, isn't it? They seem to have tons of meetings and you hate meetings. They make public appearances and cut ribbons and are frequently smiling toothy grins. It all sounds like all the things you dislike rolled up into a single entity. Plus, those people really irritate you."

Myrtle considered this. It was all true. Miles knew her very well. Myrtle said, "What if I just *run* and then don't actually fill the open spot?"

Miles gave her a doubtful look. "But what if you win?"

"Well, of *course* I'd win. Everyone knows how sensible I am. No, I'm saying that I could run, make everyone *believe* I'm going to take the seat, and then drop out of the race before everyone votes."

"What would you accomplish doing that?" asked Miles, quite reasonably.

"Quite a bit," said Myrtle confidently. "For one thing, Red would be most displeased about it. For another, I could have fun fundraising events. Of course, I'd have to give the money back when I dropped out."

"Of course," said Miles dryly. "Perpetrating election fraud wouldn't be a wise idea."

"Plus, I could really help shape the conversation at the town hall. I could make people think for once. Since I taught everyone currently on the council, I could whip things into shape when I attend meetings and make them all realize how poorly they're behaving."

"I'm sure they'll love that."

"They should view it as a reminder of how childish they're being," said Myrtle. "Anyway, I think it would be a breeze to get support. I'll have the whole of book club and garden club behind me. I could have Tippy Chambers as a campaign advisor. She loves organizing things and she's done political things with Benton before." Pasha, still sitting in Myrtle's lap, bumped her face on Myrtle's hand to remind her she was there, and Myrtle absently stroked her.

Miles arched his brows. "With Tippy Chambers in your corner, you'd be a shoo-in. But I'm not sure she would appreciate it when you abandon ship and remove yourself from the ballot.

Myrtle said breezily, "Tippy likes *fixing* things. As long as I've influenced town council and whipped them back into shape again, she won't care if I'm on the ballot or not."

There was a knock at the door and Myrtle frowned and squinted at the wall clock. "Who on earth is at my door this early? You're the only one who visits at this time of day and you're already here."

"Well, there's one way to find out."

Myrtle grabbed her cane and thumped her way to the front door, looking suspiciously out the peephole. "Oh, for heaven's sake," she hissed. "It's Erma Sherman."

Erma was one of the banes of Myrtle's existence. She lived next door and would pounce out sometimes and regale Myrtle with a myriad of disgusting health problems. She also allowed her crabgrass to spill over into Myrtle's yard and she fed squirrels, attracting them to both of their yards. Erma, in Myrtle's mind, was an irredeemable disaster on all fronts.

"Shouldn't you let her in?"

Myrtle said, "Do *you* want to start your day with her?"

Miles said, "She knows you're here you do realize."

"I could be in the shower, for all she knows."

Miles said, "Then she'll just pester you later on. You know you can't escape it—you might as well get it over with."

Myrtle squared her shoulders and warily opened the door. Erma bounded in like Tigger from *Winnie the Pooh*. Erma was allergic to cats and shrieked when she spotted Pasha. Pasha gave her a cold look before stalking outside. Erma relaxed as soon as the cat was gone. She wore a robe and slippers and a very excited expression. "Hi all!" she sang out. Erma paused, sniffing with her long nose. "Do I smell pancakes?"

"They're all gone," said Myrtle crisply. "We have breakfast very early here."

Erma looked a bit crestfallen, but then quickly bounced back. "Coffee?"

Myrtle was reluctant to fuel Erma's inexplicable hyperactivity any further by giving her caffeine, but supposed she couldn't refuse a guest coffee. "I'll pour you some," she muttered and stomped toward the kitchen.

"With cream and sugar," trilled Erma. "You don't use sweeteners, do you, Myrtle?"

Myrtle growled, "Just sugar here."

"I figured," said Erma happily. "I've noticed older people like using the basics. Real butter, not margarine. Real sugar, not sweeteners."

Miles suppressed a grin as he heard Myrtle muttering again from the kitchen. Erma wasn't a young woman either, but she liked to act as if there were multiple generations between them.

Erma unwisely continued, "Older people have real cream, too. I'm excited about real cream."

"I have half-and-half!" hollered Myrtle.

Erma's face fell before she quickly recovered. "Well, that's fine. At least I don't have to have sweetener. The last time I had some, my stomach revolted on me. I was in the bathroom for ages. It was awful, the gurgling noises it made."

Myrtle made a gurgling noise herself and again Miles worked hard to keep his lips pressed tightly together.

Erma glanced around, looking very pleased with herself. "I've been wanting to crash one of your sleepovers for a long while, you two. It was *so* much fun last time."

Miles gave her a smile. Myrtle said sternly from the kitchen, "They're not sleepovers, Erma. There is no sleeping going on here, which is entirely the point. This is a gathering of insomniacs." She walked back into the living room and thrust the cup of coffee at her unwanted guest.

"This is lovely," Erma said, giving an exaggerated sigh. "Hanging out with other people who can't sleep either is wonderful."

Myrtle grunted. She strongly suspected that Erma had had plenty of sleep and had set her alarm early so she could come by just to interfere in Myrtle's business.

"So, what's new?" asked Erma, grinning and showing off her large, protruding front teeth that made her resemble a donkey.

Myrtle didn't seem to be feeling chatty, so Miles cleared his throat and cast his mind about for something to say. "Well, Myrtle has just decided to run for the vacant town council spot."

Erma's already bugging eyes got even larger. "*Has* she?"

Myrtle looked irritated. "Certainly. There's nothing wrong with that, is there?"

In Myrtle's mind, that was a rhetorical question meant to be answered with a resounding *no*. Erma, however, again unwisely had other ideas.

"You don't think your age is a problem?"

"Age? What on earth are you driving at, Erma? Spit it out."

Erma said, "I'm only saying that maybe it'll be too much for you. Tiring. Irritating. And what if you happen to perish in the middle of your term?"

Miles winced and prepared for an explosion. Myrtle narrowed her eyes at Erma.

"I suppose there will be an empty seat. Just as there is now. The important thing is that I'm seasoned enough to provide guidance and leadership to the babies on the council."

Miles snorted. The "babies" were mostly middle-aged.

"Babies?" asked Erma.

"That's how they're acting." Myrtle sniffed.

Erma's eyes grew large again. "I just had a great idea!"

Myrtle and Miles waited with some trepidation for Erma's big reveal.

"I'm going to run for office, too!" Erma grinned her donkey grin at them, waiting for a reaction.

She got one. Miles's mouth hung open before he snapped it shut. Myrtle gave her a revolted look.

Erma giggled. "Oh, you didn't hear me! You two need to turn your hearing aids up."

"I don't wear them," said Myrtle coldly. "I heard every word."

Erma seemed immune to their general shock and disapproval of her big idea. "Isn't this great? I've been wanting to do something to be part of the community for a while now, you know. I thought about helping tutor kids, but then I was thinking about how germy kids are. Then I thought about helping with old folks, but then realized how germy *I* am."

Myrtle's glare was frosty and Miles pressed his lips together to keep from smiling. Erma was too old to talk about "old folks."

"This is perfect! See, you're full of good ideas. Running for office should be about bringing tons of different ideas and perspectives to the table, shouldn't it?"

Myrtle grudgingly said, "Yes. That's what it should be about." She was horrified to learn what new ideas and perspectives Erma could possibly offer.

Erma said with a leering grin, "It's not just old folks who have wisdom to pass along. We middle-aged folks do, too. I'm going to head off back home to make a list." She abandoned the coffee and practically skipped out the door.

Myrtle hurried over and locked her front door with a flourish. "If *she's* middle-aged, she must plan on expiring after 120."

"She did make one good point."

Myrtle gave him a doubtful look.

"You need to have a platform. I don't think you can simply run as a novelty act. If you're really running to change the behavior of the current council, you'll need to make an impact."

"Good point." Myrtle studied Miles thoughtfully. "My platform is civility. Would you like to be my campaign manager, Miles? After all, with your corporate background in finance—"

"I was an engineer," said Miles tightly.

"Yes, right. Anyway, you have skillsets that a former schoolteacher just won't have. Besides, this will be a short-term thing."

Miles said cautiously, "I suppose I could."

"Excellent! Now we need to go see the town clerk. That's BeeBee Cochran. She's always sort of snippy to me when I see her out. I think I'll enjoy telling her I'm running for town council." Myrtle sounded gleeful. "Then we need to think about where I'm going to make my big announcement."

Miles was looking a little overwhelmed. "Are we putting the cart before the horse?"

"Not a bit. I'm just trying to make up for lost time, that's all." She snapped her fingers. "I know just where we'll go for my announcement. Greener Pastures retirement home."

Miles rubbed his temples as if his head were starting to hurt.

Myrtle was on a roll. "That's the perfect place. They *love* me there. You know I always have ideas for improving life there."

"The food."

"Which is *ghastly*. Most of it is out of a can. The administration should be ashamed."

Miles added, "You didn't seem to like the activities they had on their calendar either, as I recalled."

Myrtle made a face. "Infantile! Coloring and whatnot."

"Coloring can be very relaxing," observed Miles mildly.

Myrtle ignored him. "I'll tell them a vote for me means I'll constantly be on the administration's back to fight for more input from the residents." She smiled to herself again. "Red will be apoplectic."

"Just be mindful of that blood pressure issue we were just talking about."

Myrtle said eagerly, once again ignoring Miles, "Let's go to the clerk's office now."

"Aren't you forgetting that this isn't exactly the time of day that government offices are open? They're worse than banks."

Myrtle squinted at the clock and snorted in frustration. "They're denying accessibility for insomniacs. Perhaps that can be one of my campaign issues."

"I think you're going to have to do better than that," said Miles dryly. He yawned while glancing at the clock. "Now I'm wondering if I should go home and try to take a nap."

"Isn't it too late for that? You'll have to set an alarm to go with me to the clerk's office and you'll be all groggy."

Miles said, "Are we *sure* you need me to go with you to the town clerk's office to file?"

"Of course I do! You're my campaign advisor, Miles. You should be with me during such a momentous event."

Myrtle's doorbell rang and she narrowed her eyes. "Now who on earth is that? What in heaven's name is going on this morning? I've already unexpectedly had Erma foisted on me." She grimaced. "You don't think Erma's come *back*, do you? To ask some sort of really ridiculous question about how to become a candidate or something?"

"One good way to find out is to look out the peephole," said Miles mildly.

# Chapter Two

Myrtle walked with some trepidation to the front door and peered out. She started smiling and pulled the door wide open. "Wanda! You're here so early. And how on earth did you get here?" She poked her head out the door, looking in vain for some kind of vehicle, most likely one on its last legs. There wasn't anything outside that fit that description. "You didn't *walk* here?"

"Needed to think," said Wanda solemnly.

"You must have been walking all night!" Myrtle bustled Wanda in.

Miles sighed. Wanda was a local psychic and a cousin of his. He wasn't quite sure what to make of her startlingly accurate predictions.

"Good morning," said Miles politely.

"Yer in danger," said Wanda in a level voice.

"*Who* is?" asked Myrtle. "You're going to have to be a bit more specific than that, Wanda. Is Miles in danger? Or am I?"

"You are, Myrtle," said Wanda. She rubbed her eyes, looking exhausted.

"What is it this time?" asked Miles. "There hasn't even been a suspicious death yet."

Wanda intoned, "Myrtle shouldn't run."

Myrtle said soberly, "Shouldn't run? For office, presumably. Is that because something awful will happen?"

Miles hid a smile. He could think of plenty of awful things happening if Myrtle were in charge of the town. Mostly to do with Red's blood pressure.

Wanda nodded earnestly. "You'll be stressed. Stress is bad for you."

Myrtle said, "I don't think stress has such an awful effect on me. After all, I solve murder mysteries and that's stressful."

Wanda gave her a look. "No it's not. You like it."

Miles smiled. "She does like it."

Myrtle huffed. "Like it? All I get is a sense of civic satisfaction from ridding the town of murderers."

Wanda said, "You like beatin' Red."

"Outsmarting him? Well, of course I do," said Myrtle complacently. "Who wouldn't?" She considered Wanda's words for a few moments. "What Miles and I were discussing was my just *influencing* the town council's direction and behavior. That I'd run for office, scare everyone into controlling themselves while representing the town, and then drop out. Would that be acceptable?"

Wanda carefully considered this. "Guess so," she said slowly.

Myrtle clapped her hands together. "I'm glad that's settled. Now let me get you something to eat. Do you want coffee, too?"

But Wanda had already nodded off on Myrtle's sofa.

"She's completely worn out, the poor thing," said Myrtle in a hushed voice.

Miles took this opportunity to stand up. "As I was saying, Myrtle, I'm very tired, too. I'll go home and try to take a nap. Wanda looks like she could use a nap too. Then give me a call when you're ready to go to the town hall to see the clerk." He hurried out while Myrtle was frowning in concern at Wanda, who had slumped to the side of the sofa.

Myrtle found her oldest, softest blanket and put it around Wanda. Then she found a pillow and shook Wanda awake for a second to place it behind her head.

Wanda gave her a serious look. "The rain."

"Rain? What rain? It's bone dry outside."

"Just remember the rain," mumbled Wanda before dropping back to sleep.

Myrtle muttered to herself as she turned off the living room lights and ensconced herself in the kitchen. It sounded as if the psychic was moving from regular predictions to weather predictions. But she knew better than to discount anything she said, so she tucked away the non-sequitur for future reference.

Myrtle worked on her crossword puzzle and tried to keep herself quiet in the kitchen as Wanda took some much-needed sleep. A couple of hours later, a sheepish Wanda appeared in the kitchen door.

Myrtle beamed at her. "Feel better?"

Wanda nodded and sank into one of Myrtle's kitchen chairs in a fluid motion that was distinctly Wanda. A black feline face suddenly peered intently through the kitchen window and Myrtle quickly opened the window. "Looks like someone is wanting to visit with you."

Wanda grinned and reached out for the black cat who bounded through the window onto the floor and then up into Wanda's bony lap.

Myrtle said briskly. "All right then. All we need now is a nice, hearty breakfast."

"But you done ate."

"I was just using the pronoun 'we' to be inclusive. You're right—I'm still stuffed from all the pancakes Miles made. I can't think for the life of me why he made such a big batch and why we felt *compelled* to eat them all." She groaned and put her hand tenderly to her stomach. "But that doesn't mean that *you* can't eat. After all, breakfast is the meal I cook best."

Wanda gave her a crooked smile and didn't say anything.

Myrtle busily emptied the remaining eggs out of her carton into a frying pan and made scrambled eggs. She had sausage links in the freezer and put those in another frying pan on the burner. There was a bag of hash browns in the freezer as well and she got those going on yet another burner. She frowned at everything on the stove. "I better stop here. That fourth burner doesn't work all the time and we wouldn't want to set the house on fire."

She made another pot of coffee and poured herself and Wanda some as Wanda gently tickled Pasha under her chin, making the black cat happily close her eyes.

Myrtle put a veritable feast in front of Wanda. It took two plates to hold it all, but Myrtle had the feeling that not a bite of it would go to waste.

As Wanda hungrily attacked the food, Myrtle said, "You know, I've had time for a little contemplation while you were taking your nap. I've decided that having a psychic as a campaign adviser would be an excellent idea. Much better than Tippy."

Wanda looked abashed. "Don't know what one does," she muttered in between bites.

"Well, they basically help the candidate make good decisions. I've asked Miles to be my campaign manager because he has all sorts of business background." Myrtle waved her hand vaguely to indicate all the experience Miles had that she didn't quite grasp or particularly want to. "But an adviser would help keep me straight and, perhaps, keep me safe, too. Especially since I have a talent for putting myself in danger, apparently."

She paused, looking closely at Wanda. Wanda did still seem healthier than she had in a while. She'd stopped smoking and no longer was wracked with the deep coughs she'd had for so long. Myrtle also knew she'd taken an interest in gardening and was growing healthy vegetables to supplement her diet. Wanda made a decent income with her job writing horoscopes for the *Bradley Bugle*. However, Myrtle strongly suspected that her brother, Crazy Dan, might squander that money from time to time.

"Are you doing all right, Wanda?" she asked.

Wanda took a final gulp of her meal and sat sadly surveying Myrtle. "S'pose so."

"I mean, that was a very long walk you took just to think things through. You walked for miles and miles. What was on your mind?"

Wanda shrugged. "Don't know. Felt like takin' a break from the house."

The house was a hubcap-covered shack that seemed to have a shaky grip on utilities. It was rather dark and cluttered in the interior and Myrtle could well-imagine wanting to escape from it.

"Ain't no electricity neither," said Wanda in a conversational tone, as if commenting on something remarkably commonplace.

"No electricity? In this heat?" asked Myrtle. "No air conditioning? No fans? How on earth are you getting by?"

Wanda sighed. "It's pretty hot."

"Well, no wonder you felt like a walk in the middle of the night. It must have been a lot cooler outside in the night air than it was in your home. Isn't Sloan paying you enough? I thought he increased your salary?"

Wanda nodded. "He pays good. But Dan has been usin' the money for other stuff."

"For other *stuff*? Not electricity?" Myrtle sat back in her chair at the table and stared at Wanda as if she'd stopped speaking English. "So, he's siphoning it off for other pursuits?"

"Buyin' stuff. Bought another couple of used cars," said Wanda calmly as if it was the most natural thing in the world.

Myrtle gave a harrumph. "Ridiculous. He's got a yard full of old clunkers up on cinder blocks."

Wanda shrugged again. "Likes workin' on cars."

"He's not thinking straight. Food and utilities are priorities over hobbies," said Myrtle, pursing her lips and narrowing her eyes. She planned on having a serious conversation with Crazy

Dan at some point in the near future. Still, she wasn't entirely sure how much effect that was going to have. He was called Crazy Dan for a reason.

Myrtle said briskly, "Well, you simply can't stay over at that house in the broiling heat with no electricity. It's barbaric. Let your brother roast there for a while and maybe he'll put on his thinking cap the next time he chooses buying a used car over paying the electric bill. You can stay here with me. I have a small guest room."

Wanda's eyes lit up. "Sounds good."

"All right. You can join Miles and me this morning to go to the town clerk's office so I can register to be a candidate." She frowned. "I suppose we'll need to run you by your house, though, to pick up any necessary items. I'd take you out to buy new items, but I'm afraid my own budget doesn't extend to that." She snapped her fingers. "Wait a minute. I know what we can do. We can go to the secondhand shop. That's definitely budget-friendly and maybe I can even find something there, too. Elaine has been on a coupon-clipping kick and she has a huge number of toothbrushes and toothpaste and other things she can donate to us."

Wanda looked doubtful. "Won't she need that stuff?"

"She wouldn't go through it all in a million years. Red will be glad to get some of it out of the house. Besides, Elaine told me that she was planning on donating a lot of it to the Goodwill or the homeless shelter or something. This will be perfect."

And so it happened that Myrtle, Wanda, and Miles ended up at the town hall right when it opened at nine o'clock. The town clerk, BeeBee, gave them a wary look as they walked in.

# MURDER ON THE BALLOT

It was never a good thing when Myrtle Clover came into town hall. It ordinarily meant a complaint about garbage pickup, a pothole on her street, or any number of other issues. She didn't usually come stand at the clerk's desk and this was, in particular, what worried BeeBee.

"May I help you?" asked BeeBee, devoutly hoping she couldn't. Myrtle had taught her English long ago and whenever she was in Myrtle's presence, she felt like she was back in high school. And not in a good way.

"Yes," said Myrtle, standing up proudly with her unusual entourage and said, "I would like to run for town council."

BeeBee gaped at her.

Myrtle frowned. "The town clerk *is* the individual one sees to receive the filing paperwork, correct?"

BeeBee stammered a little before saying, "Of course. We just have to make sure you qualify."

"Why wouldn't I?"

BeeBee gave a high-pitched laugh. "No reason. It's just a formality before I give you the packet. You have to sign our provided statement and affidavit. There are certain requirements to run for office. An age requirement, for instance."

Myrtle said, "Well, I assume I've met that."

Miles made a strange coughing sound as BeeBee looked even more flustered. Wanda watched the proceedings laconically.

BeeBee explained the different documents as Myrtle signed them and then she handed over a final stack of papers. "This is your nominating petition. You'll need to have ten signatures from voters to prove you're a viable candidate for office."

Miles raised his eyebrows. "Only ten?"

"You're only surprised because you're used to Atlanta, Miles. This is a small town. It doesn't take much," said Myrtle.

BeeBee continued in a rush as if desperate to get the little group out of there. "Then you'll just return the packet to me before the deadline." She paused. "The only problem is that the deadline is tomorrow."

"That's not a problem at all," said Myrtle breezily. "There will be plenty of citizens delighted to support my candidacy."

"Good," said BeeBee, looking relieved. Their conversation appeared to be drawing to a close, at least for the day. "Then bring the petition back after you've finished and submit it."

# Chapter Three

Myrtle, Miles, and Wanda walked out of the town hall and Miles said, "I guess you know what you'll be doing the rest of the day."

"What *we'll* be doing the rest of the day. After all, I'm with my campaign team."

Miles and Wanda looked glumly at each other.

Myrtle said, "I think we should go to the *Bradley Bugle* office first. I need to make sure the paper covers my campaign."

Miles said slowly, "But you aren't technically a candidate yet. You have to return the paperwork with the signatures by the deadline."

"Once you, Wanda, and Sloan sign the document, I'll be nearly halfway there," said Myrtle with a sniff.

Miles and Wanda followed Myrtle into the dimly lit newsroom at the local newspaper. Myrtle had a helpful hints column there and sometimes wrote crime stories, and Wanda gave extremely detailed horoscopes for the paper. Sloan was the editor and another former student of Myrtle's. He jumped up from his desk when he spotted her coming in. Every time Myrtle was around, Sloan somehow reverted back to high school, although his high school days were far behind him.

"Miss Myrtle," he said, shoving a pile of paper away from him as if disassociating himself from the clutter that engulfed him. He peered closer and said, "Goodness, and Wanda and Miles, too. Come on in and have a seat."

Myrtle came closer, but didn't take a seat. The seats in the *Bradley Bugle* office were all very unreliable in a variety of ways. They were swivel chairs that made surprising moves when one was sitting in them and they squeaked horribly. "We're just popping in for a few minutes, but thanks."

"More of a quick visit, then?" Sloan looked nervous. "Well, all right. It's good to see you." He paused. "There hasn't been some sort of murder that you want to write up, has there?"

Myrtle's son wasn't a fan of Myrtle being a crime reporter, a fact Sloan was well-aware of. Somehow, Myrtle seemed to get the scoop whenever a murder had occurred in the small town and managed to write a front-page story. It made Red very unhappy and Sloan always ended up hearing about it.

"Heavens, no," said Myrtle. "Sometimes I have *other* important articles for you, Sloan. As it happens, I have a tip for you today."

"Well, good, good," said Sloan, reaching back into the teetering pile of papers to find a notebook. "That's very helpful, Miss Myrtle. What have you got?" He poised a stubby pencil over the ratty-looking notebook.

Myrtle drew herself up to her full almost-six-feet height. "I'm running for office."

Sloan's jaw dropped and he quickly snapped it back when he saw Myrtle's eyes narrow. "For president?"

"Certainly not, Sloan! For local office, of course. Town council, as a matter of fact."

Sloan looked worried. "Have you told Red about this?"

"No, but he'll be able to read about it in the newspaper like everyone else. That's what a newspaper is for, you know. To spread *news*." Myrtle gave him a look as if an editor of a newspaper should be able to grasp that concept.

Miles gave a muffled sound that might very well have been a laugh as Wanda watched the proceedings with a steady gaze.

"Well, okay," said Sloan a bit gravely. "That *is* news. You're kind of a late contender, then, aren't you?"

Myrtle nodded. "I got fed up only this morning and Miles had the brilliant suggestion that I should run for office myself."

Miles gave Sloan an apologetic look, feeling rather guilty that he'd inflicted Myrtle on the local government and its citizens.

"So I'm doing my patriotic duty. I'm going to straighten out town council. There're all sorts of foolishness going on there and it needs to stop. So I'm going to put a stop to it." She paused, looking at Sloan severely. "You can quote me on that."

Sloan jumped and jotted down a few notes with his stubby pencil while Miles tried to hide a smile.

"Foolishness. Got it," he said. "What sort of foolishness exactly? There's been so much I've reported on that I feel like I need your take on what was especially egregious. Just for the record."

Myrtle started enumerating on her fingers. "There was that nonsense with the gavel."

Miles frowned. "I must have missed that one."

Sloan said, "The mayor's gavel was snatched away by one of the commissioners. She somehow anticipated this move and pulled another gavel out of her briefcase."

Miles looked slightly stunned. These sorts of shenanigans had apparently not happened in Atlanta.

"Then there was that business with the mayor not responding to public records requests," added Myrtle. "As a member of the press, I took great umbrage to that."

Sloan nodded and kept making notes.

Myrtle said, "Then there was that scuffle when one of the commissioners wanted to audio record the meeting."

"A scuffle?" asked Miles.

Sloan said, "They dove for the commissioner's phone so he couldn't record the proceedings."

"Which, considering how ridiculous and embarrassing the meetings are, is completely understandable," said Myrtle. "And of course, several of the meetings lately have ended in various elected officials yelling at each other. Completely reprehensible and a terrible example to our citizens on how to behave when we disagree with one another."

Miles gave a low whistle. "No wonder you wanted to run for office."

Myrtle frowned at him. "Actually, Miles, I'm surprised that you didn't know all of these antics were going on. You read the paper every day."

Miles looked guilty. "It's stressed me out a bit lately, so I've been focusing on the comics, the crossword, and the Sudoku."

Sloan chuckled. "Well, glad the *Bradley Bugle* can offer you some escape, anyway." He turned to look at Wanda, who'd remained quiet and was taking in the office around her. Myrtle thought sadly that it was likely cluttered enough to remind her of her home. Sloan said, "Wanda, you doing all right?"

Wanda nodded and said, "Stayin' with Myrtle for a little while."

Both Sloan and Miles blinked at this.

"Yes, we've made arrangements," said Myrtle briskly. "Wanda didn't bring her overnight bag with her, but we're going shopping as soon as we get the chance."

"Got some horoscopes for ya," said Wanda levelly to Sloan.

Sloan beamed at her. Wanda's horoscopes were the main draw for his newspaper. In fact, he'd told Myrtle before that he believed Wanda was responsible for the recent surge of subscriptions.

"That's great," he said. He glanced at Myrtle. Wanda was functionally illiterate, and Myrtle provided the transcription of Wanda's horoscopes for him. "Maybe y'all will have time to send those in soon?" His voice was hopeful.

Myrtle said, "As soon as we get my packet finished and back to town hall and after we get Wanda settled comfortably. Which reminds me; I need you to sign my packet, Sloan. You too, Wanda and Miles."

Sloan looked uncomfortable again. "Are these signatures on public record? I feel like I've sort of got a conflict of interest.

As a news guy, I'm supposed to be impartial with the election. I don't want people thinking it would affect my reporting."

Myrtle said, "Oh for heaven's sake, Sloan. Nobody's going to be digging through that packet. It's not an endorsement; it's supposed to simply indicate that I'm a viable candidate."

Sloan nodded unhappily and picked up his pen again. Myrtle opened the packet and proffered the document to him and then Miles and Wanda in turn. Wanda took a long time making sure her signature was as perfect as she could make it.

"There," said Myrtle in satisfaction. "I'm practically official now."

Sloan said, "Okay, good. I'll be sure to run a story on your candidacy tomorrow." He scratched his head. "Reckon you're setting some records in terms of candidate age. You do know who you're up against, right?"

"Royce Rollins. He has no business running for office. I taught him high school English and it was a disaster. Anyway, I don't think he's much competition at all," said Myrtle with a sniff.

"Maybe not, but he's not exactly a fun person to have a run-in with, Miss Myrtle. He likes to have his own way and it seems to me that he thinks he's already got this council seat in the bag. Like I said, he doesn't like to be crossed and he doesn't like to lose." Sloan looked worried.

"I can take care of myself, Sloan, especially around the likes of Royce Rollins. Besides, I have my entourage with me for protection."

Sloan eyed the ragtag group and looked even more worried. "You could let Red know. I mean, I know you wanted him to find out in the newspaper, but you might want to give him a heads-up so he can keep an eye on your house."

Myrtle grimaced. "Thanks, but no thanks. I don't need Red watching my house and getting into my business any more than he already is. Besides, I live directly across the street from him—I think that's enough of a deterrent." She frowned at Sloan. "You're not saying that you think Royce would do me any *physical* harm?" Her expression didn't bode well for Royce the next time she saw him.

"I'm not saying anything, Miss Myrtle, except to watch out for him and stay out of his way. That guy's mean as a snake."

Myrtle looked thoughtful. "You know, I remember a good deal about Royce as a student. I'll state again that he has absolutely no business being in local government."

Miles said, "What was he like?"

"He was a cheater," said Myrtle simply. "You're right, Sloan, Royce doesn't like to lose. If he knew he wasn't prepared with a research paper, he'd pay someone to write it for him. I caught him a couple of times. I watched him like a hawk during tests because he'd have a crib sheet written on his arm or he'd be looking at someone else's paper." She mulled this over for a few moments. "I should expose him for that. Call him out."

Miles raised an eyebrow. "When did these alleged incidents occur?"

"Not *alleged*. These were actual incidents. And they must have been . . . oh, thirty-four years ago."

Miles said dryly, "The statute of limitations for a high school cheating episode has likely been reached."

"Still, I think it speaks to his *character*. A person can only change so much. Who knows what kinds of unethical things he gets up to now? Maybe high school was just a warm-up. If he's elected, he'll have the opportunity for even more corruption." Myrtle squared her shoulders as if on a mission. "We *can't* let Royce win. Let's go get the rest of my signatures so we can return the packet. Sloan, I'll give you all the information you need later today when I formally announce my candidacy. Miles will take pictures."

Miles sighed.

They piled into Miles's car again, and Miles said, "Where are we heading?"

"Greener Pastures Retirement Home. I want to get this knocked out in a single visit. We'll go in, announce to the staff that we're putting on a special event, collect signatures, and then you'll take pictures while I make a speech."

Miles drove carefully down the street. "Have you let them know you're coming?"

"Of course not, Miles. That defeats the purpose of a surprise event. This is supposed to be something of a bombshell."

"It's sure to be that," murmured Miles.

Myrtle had made Wanda sit in the front seat with Miles and she sat there with perfect posture, hands folded in her lap. Myrtle craned her neck, looking out the windows from her new perspective in the back seat. She commented from time to time about whose yard was a real mess and who had a new car and whose cat wasn't nearly as cute and smart as Pasha was.

"What're you gonna say in yer speech?" asked Wanda curiously.

Myrtle said airily, "Oh, you know. The usual thing, but tailored to a retirement home audience. I want to assure them that I could make life better for them as they suffer under the tyranny of the administration at Greener Pastures."

"This should be an entertaining morning," muttered Miles.

As they pulled up to the retirement home's campus, Myrtle sniffed. "Perhaps the staff could do something about the grounds here. They're getting overrun with weeds and vines."

Miles glanced over. "There's just a couple of weeds poking up out of the driveway and a single honeysuckle vine on the sign that is actually somewhat attractive. It's hardly overrun."

"But right at the entrance? It reeks of a laissez-faire attitude. There's no curb appeal."

By the time Miles had parked the car, Myrtle already was taking her seatbelt off and opening her door.

For the second time that day, a front desk employee looked startled as Myrtle walked into the room. This time it was a stern-faced middle-aged woman with graying hair pulled back severely into a ponytail. Myrtle thought she looked like a warden.

"May I help you?" she asked as Myrtle, Miles, and Wanda approached the desk.

Myrtle beamed at her. "You certainly may. I need an announcement made over the intercom for a surprise event in the activity room."

The warden pursed her lips. "What sort of activity?" she asked suspiciously.

"An important political event," said Myrtle.

"Political," said the woman, making a face as if the word tasted bad. "We have policies about that. We can't have any rabble-rousing here. We have residents with bad hearts, and they might not be able to handle the stress."

Myrtle decided to change tack. "It's actually more on the educational side of things. Less political and more informative."

Miles squinted doubtfully at her.

The warden frowned. "I'm going to have to ask my manager to okay that. It sounds as if the proposed activity is in one of our gray areas." She stood up, straightening her already-perfectly straight jacket and stomped away toward some offices.

Myrtle scowled at her departing back. "This is most inconvenient."

Miles said, "They're trying to be cautious, Myrtle. You know you have a reputation here at Greener Pastures."

"A *reputation*?"

"Yes. You stir up dissent. You agitate people here," said Miles.

Wanda just looked thoughtful.

Myrtle said, "That's just silly. All I'm doing is pointing out to the inmates here that Greener Pastures needs to make changes to make them more comfortable. That's all."

Miles said wryly, "Perhaps you'd better call them *residents* and not *inmates* if you want access to the facility."

Myrtle made a face. "That warden is decidedly unhelpful. I'm not even sure if she's consulting management at all."

"Maybe you need to think about a different place to announce your candidacy. Maybe the library's special event room."

Myrtle rolled her eyes.

Miles continued, "Maybe we could convene a special meeting of the book club there and you could make your speech. They'd love it."

Myrtle said, "No, I want it to be here. We don't have all day to call up a special book club meeting—I need those signatures now. Let's wait and see what she comes back with."

The woman returned and said, "My manager said no."

Myrtle opened her mouth to give a blistering commentary on the authoritarian nature of this particular retirement community when a soft voice behind her croaked, "Tell 'em I'll read palms."

The warden peered closely at Wanda. "Wait a minute. I thought I recognized you. You're the psychic who does the horoscopes for the newspaper." Her face lit up. She glared at Myrtle, "Why didn't you tell me she was going to do readings? You threw me off with all that political mumbo-jumbo. Having Wanda here is a different story. Of *course* you can have the activity room. I'll make an announcement right now."

Wanda started unerringly loping in the direction of the meeting room as if she'd been in the retirement home a million times. "We need to git out of the way," she told Myrtle and Miles earnestly.

Miles said under his breath as the announcement came over the intercom, "What did she mean by that? 'Get out of the way?'"

Myrtle shrugged. "Who knows? But she always knows what she's talking about."

At that moment, there was a stampede of walkers and motorized wheelchairs speeding out of doors and heading to the activity room.

Miles and Myrtle gaped at the oncoming horde. "Let's step it up, Miles."

Myrtle's cane thumped as they followed Wanda to the activity room.

# Chapter Four

The room was bright and sunny, scattered with tables and chairs. There was everything from craft supplies to bingo games stacked neatly along the walls. Myrtle glanced around and said, "Wanda, we're going to need to make sure they give you some space."

Wanda nodded solemnly and Miles helped make a sort of barrier of chairs between Wanda and the door. Then Wanda settled at a small table, hands folded on the top.

The room filled up quickly and the excited chatter became deafening.

Myrtle clapped her hands and yelled out in her best retired-teacher voice, "Quiet, everyone!"

The room obediently hushed and looked expectantly to Myrtle.

"That's better. Now, listen. Wanda is making this appearance out of the goodness of her heart. This will be an exhausting process for her so we've got to have some ground rules. When Wanda is all tapped out, then that's all we're doing today. Since so many folks came in here with canes and walkers, we're going to use a lottery system instead of a line. Miles will give you each a scrap of paper with a number and we'll draw numbers out of a hat."

Miles gave her a baleful look.

"You're my campaign manager," hissed Myrtle. "It's all about sacrifice."

Miles found some printer paper and a pen and started scribbling down numbers.

"While you're all waiting for the Amazing Wanda, you'll be entertained by me regaling the group with a special announcement."

Some of the attendees looked a little leery at this.

"This ain't no pyramid scheme or something, is it?" asked an old lady wearing fake eyelashes and a suspicious look on her face.

"It *isn't*, no. Now Miles will distribute the numbers."

Miles slowly started around the room and found that the pieces of paper were quickly snatched from his hands, so eager were the participants to have their time with Wanda. As soon as he was done, he quickly pulled out his hand sanitizer and gave his hands a generous squirt.

Myrtle took the other halves of the pieces and put them in a plastic bowl and pulled one out. "Number fifteen."

There was a whoop from the back of the room and a little old man with a cane hobbled over to Wanda, plopped down in front of her, and proceeded to thrust his meaty palm at her as Wanda peered gravely at it.

"Now, while you wait your turn, let me tell you some good news. I'm running for town council." Myrtle beamed at the gathering. "I'll be representing our long-ignored age group and making changes that are sure to impact us in a good way. I'm going to make sure that town council recognizes our needs and takes action to listen to our voices for once."

"Tell them no more canned vegetables here," yelled out one woman from the back.

Myrtle took a notebook out of her huge purse and jotted down a note. She sniffed. "As I've said for many years, Greener Pastures is not taking appropriate care of its inmates."

A staff member standing at the door gave her a dour look, which Myrtle ignored.

"Are there other indignities you have to endure here?" prompted Myrtle, pen poised over her paper. "I'll pass them along to the council."

"They're slow to answer the call button," grouched an older man.

A trembly-voiced woman said, "They've thrown my hearing aids into the wash when they changed my sheets!"

The room suddenly became so loud that the staff member started looking nervous and Wanda had to lean over much closer to tell the man his fortune. Miles continued trying to take pictures, but most of the photos seemed to be of people yelling. Or of his own finger in the way of the lens.

The warden suddenly appeared, red-faced in the door. "Everyone back to your rooms and apartments, please!"

This resulted in even more cacophony from the assembled group.

"I want my palm read!"

"You can't stop us from having activity time!"

The warden blew a whistle to get everyone's attention. Then she said, as calmly as she could muster, "The problem with this activity is that it's gotten everyone way too riled up. To make it up to you, I'll make an announcement this afternoon for everyone to come back to the activity room for an ice cream social. I'll make sure the kitchen supplies all the fixings."

Everyone was mildly placated by this, although there were still plenty of grumblings. They started filing out of the room.

"Wait," said Myrtle. "I haven't gotten my signatures yet!"

But everyone ignored her as they left.

"Now what am I going to do?" asked Myrtle as they got back into Miles's car. "This is incredibly aggravating. It's the perfect example of what's wrong with Greener Pastures. Red wonders why I erupt when he talks about sending me over there."

Wanda drawled, "You could go to the beauty parlor."

Myrtle snapped her fingers. "The Beauty Box! Yes, that's a great idea, Wanda. I could just pop in and pass the document around for everyone to sign."

Miles said, "You've already made your announcement, so all that's left are the remaining signatures."

"It was a very exciting announcement, actually, wasn't it," said Myrtle, sounding a bit smug.

"Practically riotous," said Miles dryly.

"What kinds of pictures did you get from the event?"

Miles said, "Well, as soon as I stop driving, I'll show you."

He pulled up in front of the salon and parked the car. He handed his phone over to Myrtle and said, "If it's all right with you, campaign manager or not, I'm not going into the Beauty Box."

Myrtle said absently as she opened his photo gallery, "Fine, fine. It's not really a man's domain, anyway." She glared as she swiped through the pictures. "Miles, most of these are pictures of your finger."

Miles sighed. "I'm not exactly a professional photographer." He took the phone back from Myrtle and peered at the photos. "You could crop my finger out of most of these with no problem."

Miles passed the phone to Wanda. "What do you think?"

Wanda hesitantly swiped at the phone, having never scrolled through pictures on a smart phone before. She studied one of them solemnly. "This one's pretty good."

Myrtle took the phone from her and peered at it. It featured Myrtle with her pencil poised over her notebook and a roomful of red-faced, excited seniors decrying the management at Greener Pastures. "Yes, she said, "I think that will do very nicely." She looked at it even more closely. "The citizens in this picture might even be cheering me on instead of yelling complaints. At any rate, they all look very enthusiastic."

Myrtle and Wanda walked into the Beauty Box. Wanda blinked, looking disoriented. Myrtle wasn't sure if that was because of the fact that she'd never likely set foot in a salon, or because of the eclectic décor which hadn't changed in many years, despite the fact that it had a new-ish owner. Multi-colored Christmas lights were strung year-round on the walls and dangled from the ceiling. There were large posters of hair models sporting ill-advised styles from the 80s and 90s. The walls were coated in a faux terra cotta.

A young woman with black hair and pink highlights and a ring in her nose glanced up from styling a middle-aged woman's hair. "Miss Myrtle!" she called out.

Myrtle beamed at her and hurried over to give her a hug. "Kat. It's so good to see you. How is Connor doing? And your two adorable little ones?"

"They're all good," said Kat with a grin.

"Great. I was wondering if I could make a very short announcement here in the salon and then send around a little document for everyone to sign?" Myrtle gave Kat a sweet smile.

Kat looked curious but said, "Sure, my salon is your salon."

"Thank you, dear. Oh, and this is my friend Wanda. Wanda, this is Kat."

Kat gave her a friendly smile and Wanda hesitantly gave her a gap-toothed grin back.

Myrtle said thoughtfully, "Kat, what's the availability for walk-ins right now?"

"We could seat someone right away. Miss Patsy is about to go under the dryer for a while, so that chair will be available. You need a wash and set?"

Myrtle shook her head. "Not for me, no. Tell you what—I'll make my little announcement and then we'll see."

Kat nodded and went back to her client, still looking curiously at Myrtle and Wanda.

"Wanda," asked Myrtle in a whisper, "would you be interested in having your hair done? You don't have to, I just wondered if you might want to try it out."

Wanda looked conflicted. "Sort of stand out in here."

Myrtle said, "Pfft. Don't you worry about these ladies in here. Kat is salt of the earth. I taught most of the others, except for that Patsy who might be around my age."

Wanda looked longingly at the bottles of shampoos and hair treatments. "Won't it take a while?"

"Not all that long," said Myrtle with a shrug.

"What about Miles? Him's out there in the car."

Myrtle frowned. "Yes. Hmm. I'd rather forgotten about Miles. Tell you what; you sit down in the chair, I'll make my announcement and get my signatures, and then if you're comfortable with me leaving, I'll go with Miles back to Town Hall and get my packet turned in. By the time we get back, I'm sure you'll be finishing up."

Wanda's eyes lit up and she nodded shyly.

"I'll just have a word with Kat real quick and fill her in," said Myrtle striding over to quietly speak to her.

Kat immediately glanced around the room and said, "Cady, can you shampoo Wanda? I'll cut and style her as soon as I'm done here."

Cady, a cute young woman who looked to be in her early-twenties, motioned Wanda over to the shampoo station and chatted with her as she fit a towel around her thin shoulders.

Myrtle cleared her throat and said, "If I can have everyone's attention?" A buzz of loud conversation from a very deaf customer continued and Myrtle boomed, "Everyone?"

Once everyone was looking her way, Myrtle gave a speedy spiel, which was followed by applause. Myrtle was irritated with herself for not having Miles come in for pictures, but then saw

Kat had paused blow drying her client's hair and was taking snapshots.

"For my Instagram," she said with an apologetic smile.

"Can you send those to me? I'm trying to put together some pictures for my campaign."

"I'll text them to you right now," she said, getting Myrtle's phone number first.

The conversational buzz started up again and Myrtle said, "Just one thing more, everybody! I'm sending around a document for everyone to sign as part of my registration packet. If you could all sign it, I'd be very appreciative."

Myrtle handed the packet to an old lady who'd been under the dryer most of the time. She squinted at the page then took Myrtle's pen and scribbled out her name before handing it to the blue-haired woman under the dryer next to her.

"What's this for?" hollered the blue-haired woman.

"A petition," said the old lady.

"To stop spam calls on my cell phone?"

"Same kinda thing," agreed the old woman, who was very unclear about what she was signing, but didn't want to admit it since she'd already signed.

Apparently believing they were signing something to end spam calls forever, the slots were quickly filled up with signatures.

"Excellent!" said Myrtle. "All right, I'll be back soon, Kat. Thanks for taking care of Wanda for me."

Cady had just finished washing Wanda's hair and Wanda was looking relaxed and sleepy. *As well she might*, thought Myrtle, having walked all night long.

Cady led her over to Kat's station while Kat cashed out her prior client.

# Chapter Five

Miles, in the car with the windows down, had fallen into a deep sleep and was snoring lightly. When Myrtle hopped into the car, he jerked awake, startled.

"All done?" he asked blearily, rubbing his eyes.

"It was a piece of cake. Wanda's getting her hair cut and styled, so we're going to run by town hall and turn in my packet before coming back."

Miles said, "I must still be dreaming. I could have sworn you said that Wanda was getting her hair cut and styled."

"That's precisely what I said. Kat always does a marvelous job, so I'm sure Wanda is in good hands. Sometimes, when you've had a rough spell, a trip to the salon can work wonders."

Miles, who used a barber, gave a doubtful grunt.

At the town hall, Myrtle practically pranced through the door, waving her completed packet as she approached the town clerk. BeeBee gave her a stiff smile. "Hi there, Mrs. Clover. Wow, that was quick work."

"Oh, I perform well under deadlines," said Myrtle. "And of course, everyone was so eager to sign on to support my candidacy. It's been a very personally rewarding day."

BeeBee carefully checked the packet and then signed and stamped a paper. "You're good to go."

"Is there anything I should know about?" Myrtle frowned at BeeBee as if she were falling down on the job.

BeeBee appeared to be frantically thinking. "I don't think so, Mrs. Clover. Is there something I've forgotten?"

"Are there any formal campaign dates I should be aware of? Debates? Things of that nature?"

BeeBee said slowly, "Well . . . no. It's a town council seat. We don't really host debates for small seats. Actually, there aren't even debates for mayor. The newspaper editor just sends over interview questions to the different candidates and they respond and he prints them. That's the main way citizens understand where the candidates stand on issues."

Myrtle's eyebrows drew together. "That really won't do at all. I want to make sure certain issues are addressed. I want the town council to understand how poorly they're behaving and I need a platform for that."

"You could always challenge the other candidate to a debate," said BeeBee with a shrug. "I'm sure we could host it in the council room. Sloan would surely advertise it in the paper. That would be a good way to spread the news about your message." She looked a bit curious as to what this message might be.

Myrtle turned to Miles. "What do you think, Miles?"

Miles, who had been busy using hand sanitizer since he opened the door leading into town hall, looked startled and then a bit abashed for not paying attention.

Myrtle frowned at him. "What do you think about asking Royce to debate me? Doesn't that sound like a way to amplify my ideas?"

Miles nodded. Then he cleared his throat. "Is Royce the only other candidate? Because we did speak with Erma, you know."

Myrtle shuddered at the mention of her name. "We certainly did. I devoutly hope she didn't follow through on her intentions."

"Erma Sherman?" asked BeeBee. "She's already turned her packet back in."

Myrtle and Miles blinked at her.

"She's an official candidate?" asked Miles slowly.

"Who on earth signed her packet?" asked Myrtle.

BeeBee neatly stacked an already-neat stack of papers. "She mentioned that she collected them from all the different physicians she sees."

Myrtle and Miles gave each other doleful looks.

"That would fill up her page with signatures right there," said Myrtle.

Myrtle and Miles silently left town hall and got back into Miles's car and drove back over to the Beauty Box salon.

Myrtle was still muttering under her breath about Erma. "What a disaster," she said.

Miles shrugged. "I doubt she's going to win the election, Myrtle."

"Well, but I doubt she has an exit strategy from the campaign like I do, either. I'd hate to have to stay in the race to ensure people have anti-Erma options."

Miles pulled into a parking spot. "But they would have an anti-Erma option when you drop out. They could vote for Royce Rollins."

Myrtle made a face. "That's not exactly much of a choice. Some people might mistakenly think Erma is the lesser of the two evils. All I wanted to do was to run for a while and scare the council into acting like grownups. Then I'll drop out gracefully."

"You still might have the opportunity to do that. We don't know how it's all going to end up."

Myrtle got out of the car and walked somewhat distractedly into the salon. She stopped short as she saw Wanda, grinning shyly at her with freshly washed and styled hair.

"Wanda! I love your new cut," said Myrtle.

Wanda reached a frail hand up to carefully touch it as if worried about damaging it in some way. She nodded. "Kat done good."

"She certainly did," said Myrtle. Wanda's gray-streaked hair looked so much healthier with the chin-length cut and Kat had indeed worked wonders with her layering technique.

Kat gave a little bow and a laugh. "Wanda is great. You come back anytime, okay?"

Myrtle rummaged in her purse for her wallet. "I'm going to take care of this today. We're having a little 'celebrate Wanda' day today."

Kat held up her hands. "Nope. It's on the house. It was my pleasure." She said under her breath to Wanda and Myrtle, "It was nice to do something besides dyes and wash and sets."

Myrtle beamed at her. "Well, thanks so much! You know I'll be back in soon and we'll catch up."

Wanda gave Kat a smile and a thanks and then they headed out. When they got into the car, Miles said, "Wanda, you look fantastic."

Wanda blushed and mumbled a thank you.

Myrtle said, "This is turning out to be a very good day, isn't it? I think to cap everything off, we should go ahead and drop by the consignment shop and pick out some new outfits to complement Wanda's new look."

Miles sighed. He hadn't planned to be part of Wanda's makeover day.

"While Wanda is shopping, I'm going to call Royce and challenge him to a debate," said Myrtle as Miles started driving toward Attic Treasures, the thrift shop.

Miles said, "I don't think you *challenge* the other candidate for a debate, do you? You're making it sound as if you're setting up a duel."

"*Invite* him to debate me, then," said Myrtle. "And the sooner the better."

Attic Treasures was very quiet, which was a good thing. Wanda already looked a bit self-conscious being there and having a lot of other customers would have definitely made things worse. It was a fairly small store that had a few cute outfits with brightly colored accessories in the front window that the owner, Patsy, had put together. Inside the shop were clothes organized on racks by color and then by size.

Miles, wisely, had decided to stay in the car.

Patsy came over with a big smile for Myrtle. "Miss Myrtle! How are you doing, sweetie? I haven't seen you in here for a while, darlin'!"

Myrtle bared her teeth in a smile at Patsy as Wanda gave Myrtle a wary look. Myrtle was not at all fond of people speaking to her as if she were three years old. However, she was willing to overlook this and not give Patsy a crushing reply. Wanda did need better clothes and Patsy, despite her obvious inadequacies, was very good at personal shopping.

"Actually, I'm in here to help my friend, Wanda, find some new clothes. Do you think you could help us out?"

Patsy gave Wanda an assessing look and then quickly said, "Goodness, yes. We have all kinds of cute things that I just know you'll like, Wanda."

"Do you know your size, Wanda?" asked Myrtle.

Wanda froze and shook her head.

Patsy gave a careless wave of her hand. "Pfft, Miss Myrtle. No need for her to tell me. I know a 00-Tall when I see one. I don't often see one, so we have even *more* cute things for you to consider, Wanda, because no one else can wear them!"

Wanda gave her a tentative smile and followed as Patsy swiftly strode to several racks, narrowing her eyes at various selections before whipping out a few and holding them up to Wanda's thin frame and giving them considering looks between narrowed eyes. "Yes. You're one to go with more of a classic look, aren't you? Not a bold pattern, but lots of solids in neutral shades, right?"

Wanda, looking rather bemused, nodded obediently.

Myrtle tilted her head to one side. "Patsy, can you go ahead and stick those in a changing room for Wanda?"

"Of course, sugar dumplin'!" Patsy trotted off to the back of the store.

Myrtle said to Wanda, "These things are not expensive, Wanda, and it's my treat. The important thing is that we don't owe Patsy *anything*. If you don't like these clothes, we'll go somewhere else. If you like *all* of them, we'll get them all. So it shouldn't be something you worry about, okay? If you need me to tell Patsy to back off, believe me, it will be my pleasure."

Wanda slowly gave her a crooked, snaggle-toothed grin. "Got it."

"If it's okay with you, since I'm not much help in the fashion department, I've got a phone call to make to Royce to set up a debate . . . is that okay? You just be sure to give me a sign if Patsy is starting to railroad you."

Wanda said, "Okay."

Myrtle kept a watchful eye as Wanda trudged off to the changing room to see how the clothes fit. Then she pulled her phone out of her pocket. She didn't have Royce's number, but she had his wife's. She called Jenny and got Royce's phone number from her. Then she called Royce.

"Hello?" asked a brusque voice on the other end. It sounded as if Royce might be driving.

"Royce, this is Myrtle Clover," purred Myrtle. "I understand you're running for town council."

Immediately Royce's voice changed into a completely different, politicking tone. "Why hi there, Miss Myrtle. Goodness gracious but it's been a long time since I've had the pleasure of speaking with you. I am indeed running for office locally and would love to have your support."

"It's so important to have good people on town council, don't you think?" asked Myrtle sweetly. She watched as Wanda came out of the changing room in a black top and a pair of khaki pants and stood in front of a mirror with Patsy.

"It certainly is."

"Which is exactly why I've chosen to run for that seat, too." She watched as Patsy gave Wanda's outfit a critical look and then shook her head. Apparently, that one was a no.

There was a long pause from Royce on the other end. "*You're* running for that seat, too?" he finally asked.

"Yes. After all of the ridiculous shenanigans at the town council meetings, I decided it was time for a grownup to come in and make everyone settle down. Besides, I have a few issues I want to make sure get put on the table."

Royce said politely, "Well, that's just wonderful, Miss Myrtle. Goodness, I never thought my high school English teacher would be running in a campaign."

Myrtle took this as a jab at the fact that she didn't have any political experience. "I never thought the owner of a construction firm would be, either."

Royce gave a short laugh. "Business experience can come in handy in government, actually. Anyway, what was it that you called me about, Miss Myrtle? I'm afraid I don't have a lot of time as I'm driving to a meeting right now."

"I called to find a time for us to debate. It would be good to give the people of Bradley an opportunity to hear from both of us and better understand where we fall on various issues," said Myrtle smoothly.

There was another long pause. "Well, Miss Myrtle, much as I'd enjoy having a conversation about our different views in public, I just don't know if that's really necessary. Ordinarily, folks running for town council simply do interviews with Sloan at the newspaper. Are you familiar with those stories?"

Myrtle thought she detected a patronizing tone in Royce's voice. That would never do. She said sharply, "Naturally. I'm Sloan's investigative reporter, you might recall."

"Oh right, right." Still that patronizing tone. "Since it's just the two of us and since I'm really busy ... actually, I suppose we both are. Anyway, I believe it would be best to simply follow tradition in this matter and have our views run in the newspaper."

"Except it's *not* just the two of us. Erma Sherman is also running for the seat."

This was the second bombshell of the conversation for Royce. "Erma *Sherman*? She's running for office?"

"She was inspired," said Myrtle simply.

There was a chuckle on the other end of the phone. "Okay. All right, I give up. When is it that you want to have this debate, Miss Myrtle? I'll be there. You and Erma get together and set it up and I'll be delighted to attend."

Myrtle bristled at the smugness in his voice. He certainly seemed confident that he was going to come out looking very good at the debate.

"Oh, Erma is generally always free. I think this type of thing is better handled sooner, rather than later, don't you think? Let's do it on Friday evening at the town hall. I'll make sure Sloan prints something in the paper tomorrow about it."

"You got it." Royce's voice sounded a bit bored now. "Okay, Miss Myrtle, it's been a pleasure, but I've got to run now. See you Friday."

# Chapter Six

Myrtle got off the call as Wanda came out of the dressing area carrying several tops that apparently had both her and Patsy's approval, a pair of black jeans, and a pair of blue jeans. What was more, Wanda looked flushed and happy.

Myrtle settled up with Patsy at the checkout counter and then they headed back to Miles's car where Miles was diligently working on a Sudoku he'd dug up from the center console.

"All set?" asked Miles with a smile at Wanda and she gave him a smile and a nod in return.

Miles said, "I'm almost scared to ask, but where to now?"

"Back to my place, actually, after stopping very briefly by Elaine's house to pick up a few toiletries for Wanda. She and I are going to need to launder these consignment clothes before she wears them. It's probably time for us to eat again." Myrtle said this in response to the sound of Wanda's tummy growling. "Also, I'll need to send Sloan that information for his article on me tomorrow."

"An' the horoscope," said Wanda.

"So we have lots to do."

"Will you need your campaign manager anymore today?" asked Miles. His tone indicated that he fervently hoped not.

"Not unless you feel like writing horoscopes or doing laundry. But I do need you to send me the best of those pictures you took so I can edit them and send them along to Sloan."

When Miles pulled up to Myrtle's house, he said, "Uh-oh."

Red was sitting on Myrtle's front porch, arms crossed.

"He looks combative," said Miles.

Wanda croaked, "Ain't happy about you runnin.'"

"Well, that was a given. Red should be pleased that his mother is so engaged in the community. Besides, having a family member in politics could be very useful for a small town's police chief," said Myrtle with a sniff.

"All right. But just in case he *isn't* delighted and grateful at your candidacy, this campaign manager is going to head back home," said Miles.

Myrtle hopped out of the car and Wanda slowly followed as Miles drove off.

"Hi, Mama," grated Red as Myrtle came up to the house and dug her keys out of her purse.

"Well, hi there," said Myrtle brightly. "What a pleasant surprise."

Red held the door open and Myrtle sailed past him, thumping her cane emphatically as she went. Wanda hesitated until Red politely said, "Good to see you, Wanda." She smiled and shuffled past him into Myrtle's house.

Wanda perched on the edge of Myrtle's most uncomfortable chair and watched the proceedings. Red looked sternly at Myrtle.

Myrtle pointed toward the kitchen. "Lemonade, Red? Crackers and cheese?"

"You know very well I'm not here for a social visit."

Myrtle knitted her eyebrows. "Who was the tattletale? Was it Sloan?"

"Mama, Greener Pastures called me. Said you'd been creating a ruckus at their facility."

Wanda bit her lip. Myrtle said sourly, "It was hardly a *ruckus*. It was a perfectly benign political event."

"They said hosting political events was not allowed on their premises."

Myrtle said, "Isn't that so typical of Greener Pastures? Suppression of their inmates' basic rights? The Constitution allows for freedom of assembly, you know."

Red sighed. "Mama, you're missing my point. I'm not worried about what's happening at the retirement home as long as no crimes have been committed."

"Well, whether a crime *has* been may be a matter of opinion. For all we know, Greener Pastures might be raking in money that's supposed to go to their inmates' care. I mean, *canned vegetables* in the dining hall? Absurd."

He continued, "I'm more concerned about what you're doing running for political office. Do you think, at your age, that's a wise thing to do?"

"I think it's a very wise thing to do. There needs to be more octogenarian leadership in this country. It's not just a wise thing to do, it's an important thing to do."

"Royce Rollins is a tough opponent." Red shook his head. "I heard some buzz about a debate, too. He'll eat your lunch."

"You don't have to attend if you'll find it upsetting," said Myrtle crisply.

Red put his head in his hands and rubbed his eyes. He muttered something under his breath. Then he raised his head and looked at Wanda. "Have you pulled poor Wanda into your antics?"

"Wanda is here as my guest. She's spending a little time at the house with me and will act as one of my advisers."

Wanda gave Red a hesitant gap-toothed grin and Red planted his face in his hands again.

"Now, if you'd be so kind, I'm ready to watch my soap opera. So unless you want to find out if Ginger and Morgan's relationship will progress to the next level on *Tomorrow's Promise*, I recommend that you head off back home." Myrtle pointedly picked up the remote.

"There's just one more thing, Mama. You realize there's a whole financial aspect to running a campaign, don't you? Royce Rollins has a lot more money to play with."

"Don't you worry about that. I have fundraising events planned. It's all going to go just fine."

Wanda raised an eyebrow at this news of fundraising events.

As the dulcet tones of the intro of *Tomorrow's Promise* filtered through the small living room, Red hastily made his exit.

Myrtle paused the show as soon as he left. "Sorry about that, Wanda. Red just can't help himself for barging into my business."

"He cares about you," said Wanda simply.

"I suppose so. But it's all very annoying, just the same." She glanced over at Wanda. "I guess now I need to have a fundraising event planned. Something to really stand out. Something *different*."

"You got them gnomes," said Wanda.

Myrtle snapped her fingers. "You're right. I could pull them all out and have a gnome petting zoo. Invite families to come out and take pictures for a small donation."

"Whatcha gonna do with that money when you quit?"

Myrtle pursed her lips. "I'm going to have to think of a worthy charity to give it to. But until then, it's all got to look like a real campaign."

The days leading up to the debate fell into a routine. Myrtle would get up quite a bit earlier than Wanda and would finish her crossword puzzle and the Sudoku by the time Wanda woke up. Then, because Wanda had really taken to the lake, she and Wanda would take cups of coffee and some store-bought muffins down to the rocking chairs on the dock and sit and watch the sun rise. Miles would come over at some point and they'd work on a puzzle together. Miles and Wanda were especially good at puzzles and could look at a puzzle piece and know exactly where it fit into the big picture. Myrtle, on the other hand, preferred to approach them another way—by picking up a piece and turning it a multitude of ways as she tried to fit it onto numerous pieces.

Then there'd be a walk . . . frequently with Pasha the cat tagging along with them. Pasha was very fond of Wanda and stopped by often to spend quiet time with her. This had the additional positive effect of keeping Erma at bay, since Erma was allergic to Pasha and quite terrified of her.

Myrtle also spent quite a bit of time on the phone with the current town council members, informing them of better ways for town council meetings to be conducted. She paid quite a few visits to town hall to talk about her views with whomever was in the building at the time. She appreciated how cowed they all seemed as she fussed at them about the council's general and unacceptable behavior.

As the debate got closer, however, Myrtle buckled down and came up with talking points she wanted to cover to ensure her agenda was loud and clear. When the evening of the debate arrived, Myrtle put on her funeral dress and practiced her short, memorized parts.

Miles arrived to pick up Myrtle and Wanda and looked at Myrtle in surprise. "Your funeral dress?"

"It's a somber occasion, Miles. This is the most somber thing I own. This garment is full of gravitas, having attended so many funeral services."

They got into Miles's car and he started driving toward town hall. Wanda gave Myrtle a grave look. "Stuff might go off tonight."

Myrtle was still absorbed in the stack of index cards with her notes on them. "What's that?"

Wanda shrugged her thin shoulders unhappily. "Stuff might go out of control."

Myrtle frowned. "Are you saying that because you're trying to lower my expectations, or are you saying it because you've gotten some sort of vision?"

"Not a real clear one. Jest be careful. An' aware. An' don't be surprised."

Miles pulled into a parking spot near the front of town hall. There were already a good number of cars there. "Actually, that sounds like excellent standard advice before a debate. You've been putting a lot of time in practicing, Myrtle. It's worth noting that things may not go according to plans. And I know you like structure."

Myrtle said tartly, "I'm well aware that debates hold surprises. I'm sure Royce will be making plenty of counterpoints to my points. The difference is that I'm certain Royce won't be making them nearly as well. I have the advantage of having taught him English. He had great difficulty stringing coherent sentences together. Plus, I have the feeling Royce isn't taking this very seriously, which is a good thing. I enjoy being underestimated."

They got out of the car and headed up the stairs and into the brick building. The downstairs of the building was the public library and the upstairs housed the town hall offices and meeting room. Royce was just finishing up a conversation with someone and smirked as Myrtle punched the elevator button to go upstairs.

"Good to see you, Miss Myrtle," he said sweetly. Myrtle thought he had a rather cocky look in his eyes.

Myrtle greeted him coolly and walked into the elevator with Miles and Wanda. Miles politely held the door open.

Royce gave them a condescending look. "Oh, I always take the stairs."

Myrtle gave him a tight smile. "See you in a few minutes, then."

The elevator doors closed, and Myrtle seethed. "Obviously, he's planning on telling the audience I'm old and frail and shouldn't be considered a contender. He's very transparent, isn't he?"

Miles said, "So he likes taking the stairs. Maybe it's just to stay in shape. Just forget about it."

But Myrtle didn't. She carried that irritation with her as she walked into the large room where three lecterns were set up. She set her papers down and glanced around the room. There were a good number of people gathered there, perhaps out of interest in viewing a debate, or perhaps out of curiosity. Naturally, it being Bradley, she knew most of the people there.

Tippy, president of her book club, came right over to say hi. That was just as well because Royce was already engaged in loud conversation with someone from his country club and Erma was currently torturing some poor soul by oversharing her medical trials and tribulations.

Tippy, dressed elegantly in a black and white pattern as usual, said warmly, "Myrtle, I can't tell you how delighted I am that you've chosen to run. I think it's so important to have different voices and perspectives in a race."

"Yes, I do, too. So I'm guessing that means I have your vote?" asked Myrtle sweetly.

Tippy gave a quick laugh. "Oh, I can't talk about that, you know. I like to keep my vote private. Plus, it's all a little sensitive since I'm friends with Jenny."

Of course she was. Jenny Rollins was involved in almost everything in Bradley, just like Tippy was. She was also something of a clotheshorse, just like Tippy. She certainly hoped Tippy wouldn't think she had to vote for Royce just because of Jenny.

# MURDER ON THE BALLOT

The mayor stood up to convene the debate. She cleared her throat. "Ladies and gentlemen, we have a rare treat for you tonight. We don't ordinarily host debates here, as you know, but we have three candidates for the same seat and Miss Myrtle suggested this might be the best way to make sure everyone is aware of where they stand on the issues. I'm going to act as moderator tonight."

And so the debate commenced. Myrtle found the mayor's questions were all rather insipid, so she smoothly expanded on them, incorporating the indignities at Greener Pastures, the potholes on main street, and general over-development of the town into her answers. She also found the opportunity to scold the current town councilors for their recent behavior and was pleased to see them look abashed. She was even more pleased to see that Sloan was taking pictures for the paper and recording it all.

Then Royce got a question from the moderator and gave a smirking smile as he smoothly delivered a little speech about his business acumen and how well he was going to be able to manage all the details that arose with running a town. As if *he* would be the person running it. Myrtle glared at him.

Finally, it was Erma's turn to speak and Myrtle stifled a groan. She could only imagine the sort of drivel that Erma was going to spout. Sure enough, Erma quickly shifted over from talking about the traffic backups (of three or four cars) at five o'clock each day to other matters—matters unimportant to everyone but Erma.

"So, the facts are that you need someone in government who's multi-faceted and who's experienced a lot of personal challenges." Erma gave them all her biggest, most donkey-like grin. "*I've* experienced a lot of personal challenges."

Myrtle sighed. She could guess what was coming.

"As a matter of fact, I've had a *ton* of health problems and it's made me stronger in a lot of ways. Let me tell you about one of my *biggest* challenges—IBS, or irritable bowel syndrome."

Myrtle looked down at her notes and proceeded to prepare to zone out for a few minutes until Erma's oration was complete. However, she jerked her head back up as Royce gave a snarky laugh.

"All right, can you please spare us all, Erma? Seriously, this is a waste of my valuable time being here tonight. I think we all knew coming in the door who the best candidate is. My credentials really speak for themselves. What say we wrap up for the evening and head on out?" Royce gave Myrtle and Erma a patronizing smile. There was a smattering of applause from the back of the room.

Myrtle's eyes narrowed. Erma was bright red and she had a hurt expression on her face. Myrtle may not like Erma. She might avoid Erma at all costs. But Erma was her neighbor and Myrtle felt her blood boil at Royce's dismissive treatment of her.

Miles winced in the audience as if knowing what was coming. But then, he wasn't fond of public eviscerations.

# Chapter Seven

"First off," said Myrtle coldly, "we are *not* all in agreement that you're the best candidate, Royce. I for one have some real doubts about your morals."

Royce's eyebrows flew up. "My *morals*?" He gave a snorting laugh.

"Don't interrupt. Yes, your morals. I well remember you as a former student. You were so focused on success and winning that you'd pay other students to do your work for you."

"I call that *enterprising*," he said, giving the audience a simpering smile.

"I call that *cheating*. It speaks volumes about your intellect and inability to complete complex assignments. It also indicates that you don't think rules are meant for you. And you should apologize to Erma, who has certainly never done anything to you and deserves an apology for your rudeness."

Now there was more than just a smattering of applause as the rest of the room clapped for nearly a minute. There were also some snickers in the audience. Myrtle saw Red giving his mother a rueful but admiring look. She saw Sloan carefully taking notes for the newspaper.

Royce's face was about as flushed as Erma's now, but it was anger lending it the color, not embarrassment. He gave Myrtle a resentful glare which Myrtle held coldly. "Sorry," he muttered.

"Now, let's hear Erma's stance on various issues since we've both had our time," said Myrtle forcefully.

The rest of the debate finished in about five minutes since Erma had apparently not put a good deal of thought into her platform and eagerly just reiterated whatever Myrtle had previously said in a hurried 'ditto.'

The mayor rejoined them at the front of the room and closed out the event. Myrtle gathered up her purse and was about to head out when she was swarmed by a bunch of ladies from garden club and book club.

Tippy beamed at her. "Well, I have to say I'm most impressed, Myrtle! I had no idea you were such an excellent speaker."

Myrtle smiled. "That comes from being in front of a classroom for decades." She added, "On another topic, Tippy, you're so wonderful at fundraising, I might have to give you a call about my own little efforts to raise money for my campaign."

"Just call me anytime, Myrtle. I'd love to talk with you about it."

Wanda was also surrounded by folks in the room. But then, she'd become something of a legend with her horoscope, as evidenced by the mob at Greener Pastures. She was a very reclusive legend since she wasn't ordinarily in town. Given the chance to meet and speak with her, there was a crowd gathered.

After a few minutes, Myrtle glanced over and saw Wanda's tired expression. "Thanks for your support!" she called out and

# MURDER ON THE BALLOT 63

then motioned to Wanda and Miles to follow her out. As she was heading for the door, she heard Royce make a crack about the elevator behind her. She kept moving, not deigning to spare a glance behind her.

"Somebody should do something about that man," she fumed as she walked out the door to wait for the elevator.

"Hoping that won't be you, Mama," drawled a voice behind her.

Myrtle whirled around to see Red there.

"Maybe it will be. He needs to be taken down a notch," said Myrtle.

"I think you *did* take him down a notch, wouldn't you say?"

"Yes, but he apparently knows how to grow notches pretty quickly," muttered Myrtle. She got into the elevator with Miles and Wanda.

As they reached the car, there was a crack of thunder.

Miles grimly kept his eyes on the road as he slowly made his way back. "Let's see if we can make it back before the rain rolls in."

Myrtle said rather viciously, "I hope Royce gets drenched on the way out the door."

Miles said, "It doesn't really matter. What matters is how you effectively dominated the debate."

"I did, didn't I?" said Myrtle smugly. "Royce doesn't have the intellect or the focus to engage in a battle of wits with many people."

Miles got them back to Myrtle's house as the thunder and lightning crashed around them.

Myrtle said, "Miles, do you want to join us for a while?"

He shook his head. "No thanks. That was enough activity for me for one day. I'll see you both tomorrow."

Myrtle opened the door and Wanda followed her in. Myrtle said, "I'm going to put my pjs, robe, and slippers on. Then would you like a snack?"

Wanda's eyes lit up at the mention of food.

"I think I've got that good cheese and some crackers. Oh, there's that antipasto from the store, too. We can have a little feast."

Myrtle went off to get changed as Wanda pulled out the things for the snack and poured them both tall glasses of milk. Wanda plowed through the food with great haste.

"Maybe a bowl of grits would hit the spot," said Myrtle, rummaging around in her pantry for some instant packets.

Afterward, Wanda asked, "Ain't you tired?"

Myrtle shook her head sadly. "Not a whit. This is the bad thing about being an insomniac. It's going to take me a while to wind down from the excitement of the evening." She brightened. "We could play cards."

Wanda said in a low voice, "Don't know how to play."

"What? You don't know how to play *any* card games? Not even children's games like War, Crazy Eights, Go Fish or Old Maid?"

"'Fraid not."

"But you handle cards all the time, Wanda."

"Them's tarot cards. Not the same."

"No, I suppose not. All right, then, let's start simply. I'll teach you how to play Crazy Eights."

Wanda tilted her head to one side. "Thought you said that was a kids' game."

"Well, children can play it. But it's fun for adults, too.

Wanda looked a little doubtful.

"It'll be fun," said Myrtle in her most convincing voice. She really didn't want to turn in yet and cards were always relaxing for her. One of the nice things about having a houseguest was that there was someone to play cards with.

"Don't catch on well to stuff sometimes," muttered Wanda. "Didn't have no school."

"That's the nice thing about cards. No school is required."

So Myrtle showed Wanda how to play the game, which she did haltingly before gaining speed and, slowly, a sense of confidence.

When Wanda won the game, Myrtle beamed at her. "There you go! See, it's fun."

Wanda gave her a gap-toothed grin. "Play again?"

They played for a few more games. Then Myrtle tired of that game and showed Wanda how to play War. After a while of that, Myrtle glanced at the clock.

"I think it's time for me to try and fall asleep," she said, yawning.

Wanda looked crestfallen.

Myrtle stifled a sigh. "There's also a game that you can play by yourself. It'll just take me a little while to explain it."

After Myrtle showed Wanda how to play Solitaire, she trudged off to bed as Wanda stayed at the kitchen table, carefully placing cards on top of each other.

When Myrtle rose at four, Wanda was still at the table, mesmerized by the cards.

"For pity's sake! You haven't been here all night, have you?" Myrtle gave Wanda a horrified gaze.

Wanda squinted at the rooster wall clock and bit her lip guiltily.

"Okay, why don't you try to salvage a little bit of sleep while it's still dark outside. I have a few things I want to do this morning so I might be out when you wake up."

Wanda asked, "Need me to go with you?"

"I need you to take care of yourself and get some rest. Don't worry about me. I'm going to just stroll to town hall in a bit. Sleep tight."

While Wanda snored gently in the guest room, Myrtle did the crossword puzzle, fed Pasha when she pawed at the kitchen window, and ate some scrambled eggs and toast. She rang up Miles.

"Mmm?" answered a sleepy voice.

"Miles! Were you still asleep?"

Miles groaned on the other end of the phone. "Just resting my eyes."

"I don't know if you've ever actually slept this late before. It's eight-thirty."

Miles now sounded more alert. "Is it? It must have been all the stress from last night."

"Shouldn't *I* have been the one who was stressed from last night? I was the one debating."

Miles said dryly, "Yes, but you had enough confidence for both of us."

"Anyway, why don't you get ready and we'll head over to town hall? I think it would be good to have some photos of me looking presidential on the steps of the town hall."

There was a pause on the other end of the line. "Don't you mean 'looking commissioner-like?' I don't think I want to manage your campaign all the way up to the top echelons of government."

"Whatever," said Myrtle breezily. "Looking 'official,' at any rate."

"You weren't very impressed with my photography skills yesterday."

"Well right now, you're all I have unless I drag Sloan out there to take pictures and he's leery about showing favoritism," said Myrtle.

"There's Elaine. She still takes pictures for the newspaper's social media accounts."

"Most of them prominently feature her thumb. At least with your pictures I was able to salvage some of them by cropping out your extremities." Myrtle added impatiently, "We don't have all day, Miles!"

And so, fifteen minutes later, Miles dutifully showed up at Myrtle's front door. She locked the door behind them and then stared at his car. "We don't need to drive that short distance today, do we?"

"Apparently we did yesterday because I drove us."

"Yes, but the weather was rather threatening. It's all fine now. We should get some exercise."

They set off down the sidewalk. As they walked, several cars drove by and the occupants waved at them and smiled.

"I feel like I'm in a parade. Why are we so popular this morning, Miles? Is it because of my being a candidate?"

Miles glanced behind them. "I think it's because Pasha is following along behind us."

Myrtle stopped and turned around. "What a brilliant little girl you are! You want to come along to town hall for pictures, don't you?"

Pasha blinked knowingly at her and gave a gentle swish of her tail.

"You can be my mascot for the race," said Myrtle. "What a wonderful idea!"

"A mascot for a race that you're eventually dropping out of," said Miles. "Right?"

Myrtle said, "Once I've gotten everyone straightened out over there and have gotten my agenda established, sure."

Their little parade made it to town hall a few minutes later after a few more cars had gone by with their occupants waving and smiling.

"Oh no. It's Red," said Miles, spotting the policeman getting out of his cruiser.

Myrtle snorted. "I can handle Red, believe me. We shouldn't be surprised to see him . . . the police department is right here."

The expression on Red's face indicated that it was just a little too early in the day and that he hadn't had quite enough coffee to be dealing with his mother.

"Hi, Mama," he said warily.

"Hi there, Red."

"You've got business at the town hall?" he asked.

"Miles and I are taking some campaign photos," said Myrtle casually.

Miles gave Red a meek smile. Red gave him a weary look in return.

"Sorry that Mama's roped you into her nonsense," said Red. "I'm sure you had a bunch of other stuff you could be attending to back at the house."

Miles seemed grateful at this incorrect supposition.

"Well, I guess I'll just be heading into work. Got a few reports to write up," said Red.

Myrtle's ears pricked up. "Anything interesting?"

"Miz Colbert had some trouble with somebody trashing her birdfeeders. Thought it might be the teenagers next door to her."

Myrtle frowned. "Well, that sounds unlikely. I spent a good deal of my life working with teenagers, and trashing birdfeeders isn't their usual modus operandi."

"You're absolutely right," drawled Red. "The culprit was a raccoon. If she'd gone outside and looked at the tracks, she could have known that without calling me. At any rate, I trapped and relocated the little guy so he shouldn't be going after the second generation of her feeders."

Miles murmured, "Another day of quiet justice in a small town."

"How poetic of you, Miles," said Myrtle. She gestured to Pasha and said, "If Clarabelle Colbert had a cat like Pasha around her feeders, I'm sure she wouldn't have to worry about raccoons stealing her suet."

Red raised an eyebrow. "If Miz Colbert had a cat like Pasha, she'd have to worry about dead birds."

He walked in the direction of the police station as Myrtle fished her lipstick out of her large purse to freshen up.

Miles took a couple of pictures on the stairs with Myrtle leaning forward on her cane and staring directly into the camera.

"You look rather threatening," said Miles, peering at the photos.

"That's the idea! I'm trying to look menacing so that those on town council know I mean business."

Miles shrugged. "I thought you might prefer to look approachable."

"We can do another set with approachable photos. Let's move over right near the staircase where the sign for town hall is. We can include Pasha in these, if she wants to cooperate."

Pasha, who'd been watching the proceedings with some interest, suddenly bounded up to Myrtle as if she'd understood. Then she started creeping toward the stairwell, fur standing up on her back and a low growl in her throat.

Miles gave a short laugh. "I think Pasha is telling us she doesn't feel like cooperating. In fact, it almost looks as if she's stalking prey."

"Or like she's upset about something," said Myrtle, frowning in concern. "Pasha?"

She followed Pasha toward the stairwell and then stopped short.

"Miles, run get Red for me. He's going to need to stop working on Clarabelle Colbert's raccoon report," she said somberly.

# Chapter Eight

As Miles hurried off to get Red at the police station, Myrtle approached Royce Rollins's body lying at the bottom of the stairs. She realized her first impression had been completely correct and that the man was far past needing any sort of medical attention. She peered around to see if there were any obvious clues, but couldn't see anything that pointed to what might have happened to him.

She backed away from Royce's body and stood, hands folded and looking demure, just in time as Red jogged up. He stood staring at the scene and then said, "Okay, let's all back up out of the way. Miles, can you go grab that crime scene tape that's in my office? I've got to make a call to the state police and I don't want anybody else coming up on this."

It was time for the employees at the town hall building to all be showing up for work, so this was definitely a legitimate concern. In fact, as Red was speaking on the phone, Myrtle spotted town councilman Bonner Lang striding up wearing, as usual, his seersucker suit and a pink button-down shirt.

Red made a "back-up" motion as he continued speaking on the phone and Bonner obediently backed up. He gave Myrtle an inquisitive look.

"We're not going to be able to get into town hall today," said Myrtle. "Royce Rollins is dead."

Bonner's jaw dropped. "Here? In the building?"

Myrtle wasn't sure later whether she was trying to be perverse in not sharing information, or whether she simply wanted to know more than Bonner did. At any rate, she decided not to tell Bonner that Royce was dead at the bottom of the stairs and not inside the chambers. "That's right."

Bonner's face was shocked, his eyes big. "What happened? Do you know? Did he . . . well, did he have some sort of heart attack or something?"

Myrtle raised her eyebrows. "Did he have a heart condition?"

Bonner shrugged helplessly. "I don't know, Miss Myrtle. I mean, I knew Royce, but it wasn't like we were best buddies or anything."

Myrtle frowned. She seemed to recall reading in one of the many town council articles that there had been bad blood of some kind between Bonner and Royce when Royce had addressed Bonner at town council meetings.

"The two of you—well, there were issues, weren't there?"

Bonner hastily said, "Not on *my* side, Miss Myrtle. You know I always put the best interests of Bradley, North Carolina at heart. But Royce thought I should have picked his construction company's bid for a town project. It made him furious when I didn't."

"But surely you don't have the power to choose something big like that solely by yourself."

Bonner said, "I was the deciding vote. The 'no' vote. Royce said he was going to run for town council so he could be elected and spite me. I promise I didn't have any sort of ill-will toward Royce . . . all I wanted to do was do what was right for Bradley. His bid was too high and I'd heard about cost-cutting measures and safety issues at his company, too. I didn't think the town should be involved in it."

"You were here last night, weren't you?" asked Myrtle thoughtfully. "I remember seeing you in the audience at the debate. In fact, I do believe you were wearing a Vote for Myrtle sticker."

Bonner blushed. "Ah, yes. As a matter of fact, I was. I had a slew of them made up to show some support."

Myrtle narrowed her eyes. She'd taught Bonner and never thought he was a huge fan of hers after she'd failed him on an absolutely dreadful research paper he'd turned in. "You were trying to rub a little salt in Royce's wounds, weren't you?"

Bonner sighed. "Maybe. Probably so. But I never meant him any real harm." His eyes grew large. "You're not thinking I had anything to do with this, are you? These questions you're asking—was Royce murdered? It wasn't some kind of medical event?"

Myrtle wasn't entirely sure if Royce was murdered or not. She only knew that Royce had a very-clearly stated preference for staircases over elevators and that he'd ended up very dead at the bottom of one. But she knew Bonner and his big mouth. Maybe it would be to her advantage in figuring out what happened if everyone started talking about Royce and who might have wanted to get rid of him.

So she simply nodded and watched Bonner as he paled a little. "Gosh, I suddenly think I should have my lawyer here."

"Your *lawyer*? Do you have something to hide, Bonner? Besides, you're only speaking with me."

Bonner slapped his hand over his mouth as if to prevent any rash words from flying out. "And you're on the *Bradley Bugle* staff."

Myrtle preened. "I'm a crime reporter."

Bonner frowned. "Don't you have a helpful hints column?"

"Well, *yes*, but that's just something Sloan wants me to do every week. My biggest input are my crime articles."

Bonner said, "Then I think 'no comment' is the appropriate response to all of your questions from this point out."

Myrtle said, "Bonner, speaking with a reporter is your opportunity as a politician to set the record straight."

"Set it *straight*? I didn't realize it was crooked." Bonner was now perspiring in his seersucker suit.

Myrtle gave him a regretful look. "Well, you see how it all appears, don't you? A local politician with a long-standing grudge against a candidate—"

"I didn't have a grudge! Royce had the grudge!"

"This politician is clearly supporting the other candidate. Then, suddenly, the candidate has an unexpected, untimely demise. It sure doesn't look good, does it?" asked Myrtle sweetly.

Bonner swabbed at the perspiration running down his temples with an immaculate handkerchief. "What is it that you want to know?"

"Where you were right after the debate last night. What you were doing and who can vouch for it." Myrtle pulled out a tiny notebook and pencil from her voluminous purse and perched the pencil over the paper.

"I was at the debate and then I went home." Bonner gave her an earnest look. "And that's the truth."

"Are you certain about that, Bonner?" Myrtle tilted her head to one side and looked at him as if he were back in the classroom again and swearing he'd read the assigned chapter for English.

"Absolutely certain. You can ask my wife about it. I promise I harbored no ill-will toward Royce whatsoever—that was all on his side. I thought Royce was a fine fellow and that's the truth."

Myrtle's gaze on his features was intent. She seemed to be searching to see if his nose grew in tandem with his lying. "All right," she finally said reluctantly. "If you say so. But surely you have some idea who might have done something like this. You must have known Royce fairly well."

Bonner now seemed to get a bit of his sassiness back. "Well, you seemed to light into him last night, Miss Myrtle, at the debate. Are you sure you didn't have anything to do with his death?"

Myrtle narrowed her eyes at him. "Of course not."

Bonner looked abashed.

"Besides," added Myrtle, "Royce should have been the one wanting to kill *me*, not the other way around. I simply found it pathetic that he'd gone on the attack against Erma Sherman, of all people."

"Yeah, that was sort of a low blow," agreed Bonner. He mused for a moment. "If I had to choose someone who might have it in for Royce Rollins, I'd say Scotty Rollins."

"Royce's son?"

"That's right. They weren't getting along well, as far as I could tell. I was on my way into Bo's Diner just a week ago and Scotty and Royce were squabbling outside. Royce didn't even notice me because he was so caught up in their argument."

Myrtle shrugged. "There are arguments and then there are *arguments*. Lots of fathers and sons don't get along all the time." She glanced in the direction of Red who was stringing up police tape while speaking on the phone. "Some mothers and sons don't get along so well, either."

Bonner said, "This was more heated than some petty argument over borrowing the car or something like that. This had real animosity behind it. Looking in Scotty's face, it seemed to me that he didn't have a bit of liking for his father."

"Could you hear what this argument was about?"

Bonner nodded. "Sure could. It was over money and that's one of those topics that definitely can bring some hate along with it. Scotty was complaining about his father's lack of support for him."

"Meaning financial support?"

"That's how I took it," said Bonner.

Myrtle nodded and made a note in her notebook. "All right. Thanks for this, Bonner. Now onto another matter."

Bonner looked longingly back at his car as if devoutly wishing he could be safely back inside it.

Myrtle said in a severe voice, "This nonsense during the town council meetings has got to stop, Bonner."

Bonner's face fell even lower than it had already been. "Nonsense?"

"You know exactly what I'm talking about. It reminds me of a poorly-behaved high school classroom while the teacher has stepped out of the room."

"And you're the teacher returning to the room?" asked Bonner tentatively.

"Precisely. Being pleasant and professional is vital. Think of the poor example the council is setting for the citizens of Bradley."

Bonner said wryly, "The problem is that at this point nobody knows how to walk it back."

"That's why I have the perfect solution to the problem." Myrtle turned to gesture to Miles who'd been watching Red with interest. "Video the meetings in the chamber. Someone like Miles could easily do it."

Miles, hearing his name suddenly called out, looked at Myrtle apprehensively.

"Is Miles a video man then?" asked Bonner, looking at Miles thoughtfully.

Hearing this, Miles quickly joined the conversation to see what he might be signed up for. "I'm not a video man. I have no videography experience."

"You were the official photographer for my campaign announcement," said Myrtle.

"And you saw how that went."

"That's only because a riot ensued," said Myrtle.

"A riot with my thumb in the middle of it."

"At any rate," said Myrtle impatiently, "I believe the issues currently present in the meetings would completely dissolve if the meetings are recorded for public consumption."

Bonner, who'd at first appeared like he was going to be totally resistant on anything Myrtle might propose, suddenly looked thoughtful. "Actually, that might be a good idea. There are a couple of members who sound completely sour and bad-humored during each meeting. I'm usually a pretty upbeat and positive person and these folks really ruin my good mood. I've started dreading our meetings."

Myrtle nodded. "So have I and I'm just reading about them in the paper."

"Videotaping the meetings. Yes. I do believe I'm going to propose that the very next chance I get. Thanks for this, Miss Myrtle. I hope your day starts to improve."

Myrtle noticed that Bonner scooted away as quickly as he could. She was raising her eyebrows in surprise at this when she saw Red approaching her. Was Bonner hesitant to speak with Red?

Red appeared to notice Bonner's speedy retreat as well. His eyes narrowed as he watched him hop into his BMW sedan and take off.

# Chapter Nine

"Mama, you didn't tell Bonner anything, did you?" he asked grimly.

"*Tell* him things? Certainly not."

Red persisted. "I mean, did you tell him how Royce died?"

"Of *course* I didn't. What sort of idiot do you think I am? *Really*, Red." Myrtle shot him a venomous look.

"Okay, okay, just making sure." Red held his hands up in surrender.

Myrtle said, "So I'm guessing your concern about releasing information indicates that this is a suspicious death and that Royce didn't have a heart attack on the stairs."

Red shook his head. "Despite his stressful experience last night, I don't believe his heart was affected because of his debate with you."

Myrtle looked slightly miffed at this. "Perhaps it was a contributing factor."

Miles said slowly, "So there's evidence that Royce was murdered?"

Red gave them a cautious look as if weighing what to tell them. "Well, since Mama has already had an up-close look at

Royce, I suppose there's no harm in telling you as long as you keep the information to yourselves. I don't even want staircases mentioned in any way. You can say Royce is dead and you can say Royce died at town hall, but leave it at that. Yes, there's evidence that Royce was murdered. As I said, I don't think he had a medical episode. I also don't believe he stumbled on the stairs—at least, not until he was hit on the head."

"Well, in my opinion, he was overly fond of taking the stairs. Perhaps if he'd taken the elevator, this wouldn't have happened at all." Her voice was slightly smug.

Red twisted his mouth skeptically. "I'm of the opinion that if somebody wanted to take Royce out, a little thing like being on an elevator wouldn't stop him." He gave Myrtle a severe look. "You didn't seem too happy with Royce yourself last night."

"Did you see how he treated Erma last night? He was unbelievably rude." Myrtle sniffed.

Miles hid a smile. He seemed amused to have Myrtle suddenly turn into Erma's defender after so many years of avoiding the woman.

Red shrugged. "It was a debate. Usually folks aren't all that polite during the course of them." He paused. "To me it seemed as though Erma's feelings were hurt. Is that the impression you got?"

His voice was deliberately casual, but this didn't fool Myrtle. "You think Erma is a suspect?"

Myrtle, although not wanting Erma to be abused in a public forum, didn't have as many reservations about her being arrested and carted off to jail.

Red sighed. "Mama, I just don't know. How do you think Erma would respond after being attacked like that?"

Myrtle and Miles looked at each other for a moment. Finally, Myrtle said reluctantly, "Well, I think she'd react pretty much like she did last night—embarrassed and sad. I don't think she'd attack and kill the man responsible. Do you?"

Red shook his head. "It just doesn't seem very likely. I'll have to speak with her anyway, of course. I left the same time y'all did last night, of course. Did you happen to notice anything? Hear anything? Any arguments or bad words between Royce and anyone else?"

Myrtle was very annoyed that she hadn't noticed anything. She'd mostly not noticed anything because she'd still been so miffed at Royce. "No, nothing. How about you, Miles?"

Miles considered this seriously before regretfully saying, "I'm afraid not. We were preoccupied with the elevator and the weather. We wanted to get out of there before it started storming."

A car pulled up and Red said, "Here's Perkins."

Lieutenant Perkins was with the North Carolina state police. He had brown hair that was closely-cropped to his head in military fashion. His posture was always ramrod straight. He had a very measured walk and way of speaking. Myrtle's favorite thing to do was to give him a friendly, motherly hug to totally knock him off-balance. Which she did.

He gave a little jerk of surprise, like he usually did, and then settled in for the hug and gave her one back while Red rolled his eyes.

"Mrs. Clover," said Perkins, giving her a warm smile. "What a pleasure to see you and Mr. Bradford."

"Oh, it's *our* pleasure to be around our favorite policeman, isn't it Miles?" said Myrtle, beaming at Perkins.

Miles gave Red an apologetic look at the "favorite policeman" line.

Perkins said, "I'm sorry you've had such a rough morning so far. This discovery must have been very upsetting for you."

Red said, "Unfortunately, the victim, Royce Rollins, was Mama's political opponent."

Perkins tried his best to look as if the fact Myrtle Clover was engaged in politics was unsurprising. Or, perhaps, he *did* find it unsurprising. He was a very intuitive man.

"So your relationship was complicated," said Perkins.

"Our relationship was nonexistent," said Myrtle with a sniff. "Plus, he cheated in high school."

Perkins acted as if this wasn't a non-sequitur at all, giving a thoughtful nod. "Apparently, Mr. Rollins might have been something of an unsavory character?"

"Precisely," spat out Myrtle.

Miles and Red looked at each other.

Miles offered, "He was very successful locally, was involved in the community, and was quite influential."

Myrtle frowned. "He can still be unsavory, Miles. Unsavory people can live in fine houses." She looked back at Perkins. "He behaved in a quite despicable manner at the debate last night. You remember Erma Sherman?"

Perkins nodded, keeping his face carefully blank in case Erma could somehow be a friend of Myrtle's.

"Well, Erma is a complete disaster, of course. The sort of person you avoid in the grocery store if you spot her before she spots you. But Royce was *mean* to her last night. I absolutely cannot abide meanness."

Red said smoothly, "And with that, I'm going to sweep Lieutenant Perkins away. There is a crime scene to view, after all."

Perkins gave Myrtle a polite smile and followed Red off to the stairs.

Miles said, "I suppose we should go ahead and leave. I don't think we're going to get any more information here. Besides, Red will need to see about informing the family."

Myrtle and Miles headed to the car. When Miles started the engine, Myrtle said, "The family. You know, the family wasn't at the debate last night, were they? Jenny and Scotty? I don't believe I saw them there, did you?"

Miles said, "I'm not sure I'd recognize Scotty. But Jenny was definitely not there. I noticed that."

"You know what that means. She didn't support Royce. Or she was fed-up with Royce," declared Myrtle, her mind already off and running with this new line of thought.

"It might not have anything to do with a lack of support. Maybe she had a stomachache. Or maybe she had some sort of important engagement. She's very active in her volunteering, as I recall," said Miles. He paused. "Where are we heading, by the way?"

"Well, we can't go see Jenny and Scotty yet because they won't even have heard about Royce. I suppose we should swing by and check on Wanda. Maybe she wants to join us at Bo's Diner."

Miles obediently set off in the direction of Myrtle's house. He gave her a curious glance. "How are things going, by the way? With Wanda being there, I mean."

"Absolutely fine. She looks so much healthier, doesn't she? Well-rested. Except for this morning, of course. That was my fault, though. I taught Wanda how to play cards last night."

"That must have been interesting," said Miles.

"It was. She caught on really quickly. But I was sleepy and wanted to head off to bed, so I showed her how to play solitaire. When I woke up for the day, she hadn't turned in to bed yet." Myrtle made a clucking noise and shook her head.

"Wow. I never would have thought she'd be caught up in it like that."

"If you think about it, though, she doesn't really have anything remotely resembling entertainment in that shack she shares with Dan," said Myrtle. "Of course, she'd latch onto the first even vaguely fun thing she came across."

Miles frowned. "I don't think I even remember seeing a television over there."

Myrtle shrugged. "Even if they had one, how often do they have electricity? And they certainly wouldn't be able to afford cable." She looked at her watch. "Oh goodness. I forgot that Puddin was supposed to come and clean this morning."

"Well, you know how Puddin is. It's extremely unlikely that she's over there. Anyway, Wanda could have let her in, even if Puddin *did* show up."

When they reached Myrtle's house, Myrtle said, "I'll just run in and see if Wanda wants to come with us. Do you want to stay in the car and wait?"

Miles nodded and Myrtle headed inside. She was greeted by the sight of Puddin and Wanda staring, mesmerized, at the TV. Puddin started, guiltily, putting a bag of Myrtle's potato chips behind her back. Wanda looked up and gave Myrtle a bemused smile.

Myrtle could hear the sound of Puddin's favorite morning game show in the background and the audience cheering as a screaming contestant won a prize.

"Puddin, what's going on in here?" Myrtle put her hands on her hips.

Puddin's pasty-white face was sullen. "Just showin' Wanda my game show. Figured maybe she needed to go on one of them shows."

"Why on earth should she go on a game show?" Myrtle couldn't think of any less-likely candidate for a Hollywood game show than Wanda.

Puddin stared at Myrtle as if she was very, very dim. "Because she can see the future."

Myrtle frowned. "Does that help with knowing trivia? I don't think it does."

Puddin glared at her. "It don't hurt!"

Wanda seemed to be completely entranced by the game show, at any rate. Fortunately, a commercial came on right at that moment and Myrtle was able to briefly win her attention. "Wanda, would you like to go to Bo's Diner with Miles and me?"

Wanda hesitated. She might have blushed a little.

Myrtle said, "Or have you eaten already? Perhaps you had breakfast with Puddin?"

Puddin pushed the bag of chips further behind her. There was a distinct crunching sound as the chips were crushed into bits.

Myrtle didn't want to create a dilemma for Wanda. She had enough of those in her everyday life. "How about this—I'll pick up some take-out for you for lunch. Miles and I will eat breakfast and I can get some hot dogs to-go for you for later. Does that sound good?"

Wanda nodded, looking relieved. "Thanks, Myrtle." Then she furrowed her brow. "You might run across somebody at the diner you need to talk to."

Myrtle gave her a big smile. "Excellent. All the more reason for me to head on my way." Also, the commercial break was nearly over and she anticipated losing both Puddin's and Wanda's attention. She said severely to Puddin, "You need to get to work, since you're here. There's dust everywhere. My baseboards need cleaning, too."

Puddin said casually, "My back's thrown out. Them baseboards is gonna have to wait."

Myrtle gritted her teeth. "Well, I'm sure your back won't object to the dusting, vacuuming, and other cleaning that needs to be done around here."

Wanda pulled her attention away from the game show with some difficulty. "Myrtle, I'll git those baseboards for ya."

Myrtle shook her head. "You're a guest, Wanda. That's not your job."

"Might as well put me to work a little," she said with her gap-toothed grin.

Puddin said, "Remember, you're gonna owe me some money."

"No. You're here because I paid you once and you had to leave because of some perceived emergency. You owe *me*."

Puddin scowled.

Myrtle headed back to Miles's car.

"No Wanda?" he asked.

"We're going to pick up take-out for her while we're there. Puddin has totally corrupted her. They're in there watching game shows."

"Sounds likely," said Miles as he drove toward the diner.

"Wanda did say that we were going to see someone at the diner that we needed to speak with. I'm wondering who that might be," said Myrtle with a frown. "Hopefully we'll be able to tell who it is on sight. Otherwise, it would be awkward walking up and talking to a whole bunch of people who end up *not* being important."

"Plus, we might look very silly doing it." Miles gave a small shudder at the thought of questioning everyone eating their breakfast at the diner.

Myrtle said, "We wouldn't. People forgive senior citizens. It's our superpower. They'd simply think we were being friendly."

"Or senile. Which, speaking as your campaign manager, wouldn't be very helpful for your bid for the town council seat."

Myrtle snorted. "Everyone knows I've got all of my marbles."

"And then some," muttered Miles. "I think perhaps you've swiped other people's marbles along the way."

The diner was very busy, as it usually was. Miles had to make a loop twice to find a parking spot and was finally reduced to creeping along behind a woman who seemed to be heading to the parking lot. He quickly took her spot as soon as she backed out.

As soon as they entered the diner, Myrtle was already scanning the restaurant to see who might be important to speak with.

"Surely Lucy Williams isn't important," she muttered. She glared at the unaware old woman who was taking a large bite of a biscuit. "She only *thinks* she's important. Those are two entirely different things."

Miles said, "Sloan is over there."

Sloan certainly was. He was hastily finishing up his breakfast and taking wary looks in their direction. When he saw Myrtle and Miles had noticed him, he blushed scarlet and gave a hesitant wave.

Myrtle pursed her lips. "I hardly think Wanda would believe speaking with Sloan is important. Of course, it's important for me to notify him about my article. Otherwise, I can't see any good in speaking with him on this particular morning."

"What article?"

"The one I'm writing about Royce's death, of course! Pay attention, Miles."

Myrtle continued scanning the room, noting and dismissing all sorts of people. Then she grabbed Miles's sleeve. "There's Scotty Rollins."

Miles shifted uncomfortably and started shaking his head. "No way. He probably doesn't even know about his dad. We *can't* go over there and speak with him, Myrtle."

"Wanda said it was important." Myrtle's voice was stubborn. "I'm not going to traumatize the young man, you know. I'm simply going to feel out what he *does* know and then casually talk to him about things."

The hostess told them they could sit wherever they wanted. Myrtle said, "Okay, we need to split up. You go sit at that table near Scotty so no one else gets it. I'll hurry over and tell Sloan about the article."

Miles reluctantly walked over to the empty table beside Scotty and Myrtle approached Sloan, who looked nervous.

"Didn't you like what I wrote about the debate last night?" he sounded breathless.

Myrtle said, "Oh, it was just fine. Except for the two typos."

Sloan blushed again.

"I wanted to let you know to expect an article from me later today," said Myrtle briskly.

Sloan knitted his brows. "Today? It's not political is it, Miss Myrtle? I can't be showing favoritism between candidates. Otherwise, I'll have to give Royce Rollins equal time."

"Well, that will be difficult to do," said Myrtle dryly. "You haven't heard? I thought the editor of the newspaper surely would have found out. Or that Bonner Lang would have told half the town by now." She dropped her voice to a stage whisper. "Royce is dead. Murdered last night after the event."

Sloan's eyes were huge. "You're kidding."

"Of course I'm not! I wouldn't kid about something like that, for heaven's sake. Anyway, I'll have more information for you later."

"And Wanda's next horoscope?" asked Sloan hopefully.

Myrtle gave him a disappointed look. "Yes, all right. But you could show a little more excitement over my story, Sloan."

"Yes, yes. Sorry." Sloan looked repentant.

# Chapter Ten

Myrtle swiftly joined Miles back at the table, hoping Scotty hadn't taken it into his head to finish his breakfast and head on his way. She was relieved to see him still there, finishing up some scrambled eggs. Miles was looking increasingly uncomfortable as Myrtle approached.

Myrtle ignored Miles and quickly said, "Hi, Scotty. I'm Myrtle Clover, I'm not sure if you remember me. I'm running against your dad for the town council spot."

Scotty was in his early twenties and seemed to have an issue against shaving. He had a half-formed scruffy beard. He was thin and even when sitting down seemed to be very tall. He said laconically, "Then you're going to have a pretty easy time getting elected. Dad is dead. You might not have heard."

Miles froze, menu in hand. Myrtle took a deep breath. "Goodness," she said. Then, "I'm so sorry, Scotty. He seemed very well last night."

Scotty shrugged. "That's what happens when you're murdered. You're fine one second and dead the next."

This casual attitude gave Myrtle pause. "May I . . . well, do you mind if I sit down with you for a second, Scotty?"

He gestured to the chair across from him and Myrtle sat gingerly in it. Scotty took another bite of eggs and looked thoughtfully at Myrtle as if trying to figure her out. Myrtle was trying to figure *him* out on the other side of the table.

Myrtle cleared her throat. "So, again, I'm so sorry. Miles is sorry, too."

They looked over at Miles at the table next to them. He quickly put the menu down and gave Scotty a small smile.

"This must have come as a terrible shock to you," said Myrtle, the faintest note of doubt in her voice. It didn't seem to come as a shock at all, considering how Scotty was plowing into his breakfast. But she was aware that different people handled grief in different ways. Scotty's way was apparently gorging himself on food.

Scotty considered this. "Well, of course it was a *surprise*. I mean, I had no idea Dad was dead when I woke up this morning. But the police actually sent someone over very quickly. I guess they were worried Mom and I would find out from somebody else if they didn't tell us first. I don't know if I'd really call it a 'shock', though. Dad had a talent for making people upset."

Myrtle said gingerly, "Did he make you upset sometimes, too?"

"No. No, Dad made me upset *all* the time. That doesn't mean I'm not sorry he's gone. But it sure doesn't mean that I had anything to do with his death. But after the police told Mom and me, my first reaction was that I wanted to get out of the house and get something to eat." Scotty shrugged. "Maybe that's just my way of dealing with bad news."

"Did the police offer any information about what happened?" asked Miles.

Scotty shook his head. "Not really. They just called it a suspicious death. They mostly seemed really focused on trying to find out what I was doing last night." He snorted. "Guess they thought I might be involved."

"What did you tell them?" asked Myrtle.

"The truth. I was at home with my mom. It was pretty nasty weather last night and I was glad to stay inside."

Myrtle asked, "Your father wasn't upset that you weren't going to the debate? Or that your mom wasn't?"

Scotty shrugged. "He didn't seem to be. He knew politics wasn't really our area of interest. I think he was just glad to be out of the house and away from Mom and me. You know how families can get on each other's nerves."

"It must have been difficult having two men in the same house. At least . . . are you living with your family now?" asked Myrtle.

This seemed to be a sore spot. Scotty winced a little but didn't deny still living at home with his parents. "Dad and I got along just fine. We were just two completely different people with different ways of looking at things. But I've always been proud of him, of course. Everyone respects him. Respect*ed* him. He was a self-made man—he didn't come from money."

To Myrtle, it seemed as if these were well-rehearsed lines that Scotty had recited numerous times. She wondered what sort of relationship they'd actually had. There was a look of mild distaste on his face as he spoke of Royce.

"Your mother must have been worried sick when your dad didn't come home last night," said Myrtle. "Is that when the police were notified?"

Scotty shook his head. "Mom and Dad have separate rooms." He shrugged. "Dad snored and Mom is a light sleeper. Dad was a night owl and Mom is always up really early. It worked out better for them to sleep in different bedrooms. So she wouldn't have known he didn't come home last night and wouldn't have realized this morning that he was still out."

Miles said carefully, "You mentioned that your dad had a gift for making people upset. Was there anyone in particular that you were thinking of?"

Scotty gave Myrtle and Miles a tired grin. "Hey, are you two investigating this? That's pretty wild."

"I work for the newspaper," said Myrtle, looking smug.

"Got it. Okay, well, this obviously isn't on the record, then. Because that would be libel, wouldn't it?" asked Scotty.

Myrtle nodded. "I wouldn't be able to print something like that. But it helps with putting the pieces of the puzzle together. I'd like to find out who did this to your dad."

"In that case, I'll give you a name. But just a first name, since I don't really know this guy, aside from the fact that he kept following my dad around. His name is Foley. He's like some kind of down-on-his-luck guy. He's always showing up and trying to get my dad to loan him money or something."

"Loan him money?" asked Myrtle slowly. "That seems a strange thing for him to do. Is he related?"

"Not as far as I'm aware." Scotty snorted. "Anyway, even if he was, he's not the sort of family that my family would claim.

I don't know—maybe he wasn't trying to get a loan, maybe he was trying to get a break on money he owed Dad. Either way, he always seemed upset whenever Dad wouldn't give him any. Because he *didn't* give him any." He looked at his watch. "Sorry, but I should be getting back home and helping Mom."

"Please pass along our condolences to her," said Myrtle. "Miles and I will be coming by tomorrow with some food for her."

Scotty gave them both a quick smile and then headed up to the front to pay for his meal. Myrtle sat down across from Miles.

"Wanda was certainly right. We found someone important to speak with," said Myrtle.

The waitress came by and took their order. When she'd left, Miles said, "Who's this Foley? I don't think I've come across him."

"Funny enough, he's working for Dusty right now."

Miles gaped at her. "Working for *Dusty*? Does Dusty even do enough work to qualify for hiring an employee?"

Myrtle shrugged. "I thought it was sort of silly, myself. But Dusty has him doing the weed-trimmer and the blower while Dusty runs the mower. It does make things go a little faster. Dusty told me last week that Foley had fallen on hard times and he was helping him out by giving him a job helping him with lawns."

"I'd be very interested in seeing how that partnership goes."

"Oh, it's doomed, I'm sure. Last week, Dusty spent the whole time fussing at Foley for doing things 'wrong.' Which is hilarious. You'd think Dusty was the exemplary yardman from the way he was talking. Anyway, we should eat up here, get Wanda's takeout, and head home. If Puddin is at the house now, that means Dusty and crew will be doing my yard before picking her up. We'll have the chance to ask Foley a few questions about his thoughts on Royce and why he was bugging him for money."

"Sounds like fun times," said Miles dryly.

After eating, they headed back to Myrtle's house. Apparently, Wanda had managed to pull herself away from the game shows and was scrubbing diligently at the baseboards with what appeared to be one of Puddin's rags. Puddin was sullenly slopping dust around with a dust cloth.

Myrtle said, "Wanda, you need to stop doing that and let Puddin take a whack at it."

Puddin glared at her. "Told ya my back was thrown."

"Okay, then. Wanda, you need to stop, period. It looks like you got the baseboards that were the most scuffed-up, anyway."

Puddin happily tossed her dust cloth on the floor and Myrtle said, "Not you, Puddin! You're *supposed* to be cleaning."

Puddin gave her a spiteful look. "Time to vacuum anyway."

Myrtle was convinced that Puddin chose to vacuum whenever Myrtle was trying to have a conversation. And that she continued pushing the vacuum around far past any time when she might actually still be sucking dirt up off the floor.

"Fine. Miles, Wanda, and I will go sit outside in the backyard while you're vacuuming. I do have one question for you, Puddin. Is Dusty coming by to do my yard in a few minutes?"

Puddin shrugged. "Ain't Dusty's keeper."

Myrtle kept a careful leash on her temper. "I wasn't trying to imply that you were. I simply wanted to know if he's coming and if he'll have his new assistant with him."

Puddin said scornfully, "That Foley?"

"You don't like him?"

Puddin shrugged again, this time more expressively. "He makes Dusty mad. Can't work the equipment right."

"And Dusty is such an exceptional yardman and perfectionist." Myrtle rolled her eyes.

Puddin squinted at her. "Don't like it when you don't speak English."

"*Anyway*, is he coming?"

"Who?" asked Puddin.

"*Foley*." Myrtle said this through gritted teeth.

"Don't know. Like I said, I ain't Dusty's keeper." Puddin swept out of the room to get the vacuum out of the closet.

Miles said, "I can tell by the color in your face that your blood pressure is up, Myrtle."

"My blood pressure is perfect, like I said. *Red* has the blood pressure issue. This is just plain, old-fashioned irritation."

Puddin started up the vacuum with a roar and Miles, Wanda, and Myrtle escaped to the back yard.

"I'd say we could all sit out on the dock and watch the water, but I suppose we need to stick around up here until we can speak with Foley. If Foley's even going to be here. It's all utter nonsense, all the time. I constantly feel as if I've wandered through the looking glass whenever I'm around Puddin," growled Myrtle. Then she snapped her fingers. "Wanda, I totally forgot. Your lunch is on the table in there, if you're ready for it. That's what happens whenever I'm with Puddin—she makes me distracted."

Wanda braved the vacuum and Puddin's ferocious pushing of it to get the bag of fries and hotdogs. Then the three quietly sat outside for a few minutes as Wanda consumed the entire lunch.

Wanda, rather daintily considering how she'd wolfed down her food, dabbed at her mouth with the napkin. Then she said, "You got the information you needed at lunch?"

Myrtle grinned at her. "You make me feel like I'm in a spy novel, Wanda. Yes, I did. Miles and I spoke with Scotty Rollins, Royce's son. I got the clear impression that he wasn't much of a fan of his father, despite what he said. He's the reason we're waiting so patiently for Dusty and Foley's arrival—Scotty said that Foley was haranguing Royce for money. We wanted to ask him about it. Plus, I want to tell Dusty to put the gnomes out."

Miles gazed around them. "But the gnomes *are* out. Even in the backyard."

"Yes, but not *all* of them. And I want that monster gnome out in the front."

"That's a little excessive, isn't it?" asked Miles slowly.

"Not a bit. Wanda and I had a wonderful idea earlier to use the gnomes for a dual-purpose. So I won't only irritate Red by having them all crowded in the yard, but I can host a sort of petting zoo for the gnomes. Parents can bring their kids to have their pictures taken. All for a small campaign donation that I will contribute to a worthy charity after I drop out of the race."

Miles said, "I certainly hope you're not planning for me to be the photographer for this fundraiser. My picture-taking days are over."

"I'm sure I can get someone else to help." She tilted her head to one side. "I think I hear Dusty's truck."

Dusty's truck did indeed have a very distinctive sound to it, rather like a dump truck spilling its load. It was fond of backfiring, too.

Sure enough, a few minutes later, Dusty shuffled around the side of the house. "Puddin says you wanted ter talk to me?" He didn't look very pleased at the thought.

"Yes. If you could please remove the remainder of the gnomes from the storage shed and put them in the front yard?"

Dusty scowled at her. "Ain't no room for more gnomes."

"Sure there is. Just squash them together. I'm planning an event."

Dusty scratched his head. "Can't mow with more gnomes out."

"Just use the weed trimmer to get around them a little. Oh, and be sure to blow the driveway and front walk off since I'll have people by."

Dusty muttered to himself under his breath.

"While you're doing that, I wanted to have a word with Foley," said Myrtle.

Dusty glared suspiciously at Foley and he gave Dusty a hang-dog look and a shrug as if to say he had no idea why this elderly woman wanted to speak with him. He was a hollowed-out man with shaggy work clothes and a five o'clock shadow.

"Whatcha need to talk to him for?" growled Dusty.

"That's between Foley and me," said Myrtle severely.

Dusty stomped away toward the storage shed, his muttering fortunately getting fainter and fainter as he went.

Foley gave Myrtle, Miles, and Wanda an anxious look as if he was facing a tribunal of some kind. He attempted to clear his throat, which led to a small coughing fit. Wanda gave him a sympathetic look. She'd kicked a smoking habit herself and had mostly conquered the lingering cough she'd had.

"You wanted to see me?" Foley asked in a meek voice.

"Yes," said Myrtle. She paused, trying to figure out how best to leap into the subject as Foley looked nervously over at Dusty who was lugging out gnomes and looking annoyed. "You've been helping Dusty out, I see," she finally said.

Foley nodded. "I done fallen on bad times and Dusty's lettin' me help him out."

"Well, I'm very sorry to hear about your hard times. As a matter of fact, I was recently speaking with someone and they mentioned something about your financial troubles. They said they might intersect somehow with Royce Rollins."

Foley lifted both of his hands up and turned rather pale. "Ain't had nothin' to do with his death."

"Calm down, Foley. I never said you did. I was simply trying to get a better picture of who Royce Rollins *was*. He was my rival candidate for town hall, you may remember."

Foley knit his eyebrows together in the manner of someone trying to retrieve a memory that didn't exist.

"Anyway, were you trying to extract money from Royce Rollins in some way?" asked Myrtle.

Foley, already something of a sad sack, seemed to fold down even further into himself. He scuffed his foot through some pebbles. "Just wanted him to forgive some debt."

"You owed him money?"

Foley nodded miserably. "Done lost at poker too much."

Miles said, "Royce was a gambler?"

"I guess. Anyways, he gambled with cards," said Foley. He took a deep, steadying breath, which made him dissolve into another coughing fit.

They waited patiently for him to stop coughing. Foley finally continued, "Then my car done broke. Got to have money to get it fixed. Lost my job because I couldn't get to work." He shrugged again at his remarkable bad luck.

Myrtle said, almost to herself, "I suppose, since Royce is dead, your debt is erased."

# Chapter Eleven

Foley looked a bit panicky again. "Got nothin' to do with that, like I said."

"I know. Maybe an alibi would help, just in case someone else asks you about it. Where were you when Royce was killed?"

"Don't know when he was killed, do I? But that was when I was at the garage tryin' to get my car fixed."

Miles asked, "Did they fix it?"

Wanda croaked, "No money."

Foley gave Wanda an admiring look. "That's right. Yeah, they could fix it, but I couldn't pay for it. Still sittin' at the garage." He glanced back at Myrtle. "Called Dusty an' he had to pick me up since the car is broke for good."

Myrtle nodded. "Now someone mentioned seeing you hanging around Royce quite a bit."

Foley made a face. "Don't hang around him. Wouldn't have nothin' to do with him!" He spat on the ground, which Myrtle took as a dramatic indicator of Foley making an emphatic statement. Then she realized he was simply spitting out his chewing tobacco.

"Well, maybe you have some idea who might have wanted to get rid of Royce. It sounds as if you did spend some time in his vicinity, despite your strong sentiments about him."

Foley gave her nearly the same squinting look Puddin gave her when she wasn't quite sure what Myrtle was getting at.

Wanda translated. "Know who did it?"

Foley gave her another appreciative look before scratching his head in thought. "Let's see. Right after that last poker game, I was gonna head home. Heard Royce get a phone call. Royce, he thought he was by hisself but then he never paid me much attention no-how. He was cooing on the phone." He gave Miles a meaningful look as if Miles was the only one present who might understand.

Miles frowned. "You mean he was speaking with a woman? A woman who wasn't his wife?"

Foley pointed at Miles. "Got it in one."

Myrtle said, "So he wasn't speaking with Jenny. Do you know who he was talking to?"

Foley considered this. "Christy? Naw. Cindy. That's it. Wife of that fellow who owns the garage where my car's at."

"Cindy Cook?" asked Myrtle.

"That's her. I seen 'em together, too. I was in the grocery store one day and thought they looked pretty cozy. Canoodling with each other."

Myrtle said thoughtfully, "Well, that's very interesting. As a matter of fact, the two of them dated in high school."

"How *do* you remember things that happened that long ago?" asked Miles.

"It's a gift."

Dusty, still out lugging gnomes around, cleared his throat loudly and in a very annoyed way. Foley shot another anxious look in his direction.

Miles said, "Perhaps we should let Foley get back to work."

Myrtle gave him a distracted look. "What? Oh, okay."

Foley slumped a little in relief and took a few steps in Dusty's direction before Myrtle said, "You don't gamble still, do you?"

"Ain't got no money," said Foley with a shrug. "It were just a hobby, not a habit."

Myrtle watched as he grabbed a gnome from the storage shed and went around the corner of the house.

"I don't think I hear the vacuum anymore," said Miles.

"That's one of the irritating things about Puddin. She lies in wait. You'll *think* she's done with the vacuuming and then as soon as you go inside, she'll practically assault you with it. Why, do you want to go back inside?"

Miles said, "I just feel bad watching these guys working so hard while I'm sitting here in a chair."

"I'm *paying* them to do it. It's not like they're putting gnomes around the yard out of the goodness of their hearts. But we can try to sit inside and see what happens." Myrtle turned to Wanda. "You and I need to work on your horoscopes."

"You're goin' down to see Sloan," said Wanda.

"That's right. I want to give him my story about Royce and your horoscope at the same time."

Miles said, "Don't you usually just email him the articles? Surely, there isn't any need to walk down there again." He sounded personally resistant to the possibility of spending more time with Sloan.

"I do, but I'd like to talk to him about Foley. Sloan hangs out in that drinking and poker-playing underworld and I want to hear what he has to say about all of this. Do you want to come with me?"

"I was actually fancying a nap after that breakfast," said Miles.

"A nap? It's not even noon yet."

"Naps aren't permitted before noon?" asked Miles.

"Not unless you're ill."

"Then I'll just rest my eyes," said Miles.

"A euphemism for napping. That's fine, but don't be surprised when you're awake all night tonight," said Myrtle vindictively.

Miles shrugged. "I'm never surprised when I'm awake all night."

"I'll go with you to see Sloan," said Wanda.

Myrtle beamed at her. "Thank you, Wanda."

Miles went back to his house to rest his eyes. Puddin, fortunately, had moved on from vacuuming to a much-quieter cleaning activity so Wanda and Myrtle could go inside and work on the article and the horoscope before setting back downtown to the newspaper office.

It was a little after noon by then and when they walked in Sloan had his feet up on his cluttered desk and was delving into a large bag of fast food. He tossed the bag away guiltily when Myrtle and Wanda entered as if to dissociate himself from the unhealthy food. "Miss Myrtle! Wanda! What a surprise."

"I know—we've already been here today. But I wanted to personally deliver my article and Wanda's horoscope."

"Well, that's very nice," said Sloan in a tone suggesting that it wasn't really at all as Myrtle brought him the two documents and laid them down on the top of one of the stacks on his desk.

"I also wanted to ask you some questions," said Myrtle severely, making Sloan look even more fidgety and anxious than he did before.

"Okay, shoot," said Sloan, bracing himself for the onslaught.

"First off, do you know Foley Hardy?" asked Myrtle.

Sloan blinked in surprise. Whatever direction he'd thought this inquisition would go, this wasn't one he'd considered. "Sure, I know Foley."

"What's your take on him?"

Sloan tilted his head to one side as if that helped him come up with a quick assessment of someone he'd never thought much about. "Well, he's nice enough. He's at the bar pretty frequently." He blushed as if realizing that put *him* at the bar pretty frequently, something he'd rather his former English teacher didn't know.

"Is he just hanging out at the bar? What else do you know about him?" asked Myrtle impatiently.

Wanda hid a smile as Sloan started to look more anxious, realizing he wasn't delivering whatever information Myrtle wanted.

"Well, sometimes he shoots pool," offered Sloan in a hopeful tone. His face fell when Myrtle also seemed dissatisfied with this answer.

Wanda drawled, "Does he gamble?"

Sloan lit eagerly on this question. "Yes! As a matter of fact, he does. Mostly poker, but I think he also bets on football games and horse races and stuff like that. I don't think he wins a lot, either. He always seems short on cash."

"He played with Royce Rollins?"

"Sure. He played pretty often with him I think. The only reason I know that is because Royce played all the time. I bet it got on his wife's nerves. She doesn't look like the gambling type or the type that would accept it."

Myrtle said, "I don't really know Jenny Rollins very well, do you?"

Sloan, eager to please but not wanting to get in over his head, said cautiously, "I wouldn't say I knew her *well*, no. But I've seen her around from time to time. I don't think she was real excited about Royce running for office, either."

"Lots of that goin' around," said Wanda, thinking about Red.

Myrtle said, "What made you get the impression Jenny wasn't happy about Royce running?"

Sloan said, "Oh, I asked him a question near the beginning of his campaign. It wasn't really a hardball question, but it wasn't a softball question, either. Jenny wasn't at all happy about it. She scowled at me and told me that Royce was too busy to answer any other questions. Then she hustled him away."

"So she was very protective of Royce," said Myrtle. "I'm sure she's not taking the news of his death at all well, then. I'll have to bring Jenny a casserole tomorrow."

Wanda and Sloan shared a meaningful look.

"Was there anything else you wanted, Miss Myrtle?" asked Sloan. His tone indicated he devoutly hoped not. It indicated that the mention of Myrtle cooking made him even more nervous.

"That was everything, I think. You've got the horoscopes and the article. Thanks, Sloan."

As Myrtle and Wanda left, Sloan watched their exit with relief.

# Chapter Twelve

"Do you feel up to a little walk, Wanda? We don't have our driver right now, so it'll mean a bit of exercise."

"Goin' to the garage?" asked Wanda.

Myrtle smiled at her. "If you're up to it. It's very handy having a psychic around. It means I have a lot less explaining to do. We'll go see Preston Cook. He owns the garage and would have spoken with Foley about his broken car."

"An' he's married to the woman who Royce was talkin' to on the phone," added Wanda.

"You're a natural sidekick," said Myrtle, sounding pleased. "Yes, that too. As I mentioned, I taught all these folks back in the day. At the time, Preston was a football hero and Royce . . . was not. Cindy and Royce had been an item until Cindy started dating Preston. They married young, as I recall. Now it sounds like Royce might have gotten Cindy back, at least briefly. I don't think Preston is the kind of man who would have taken kindly to that."

Wanda turned to look at Myrtle as they slowly made their way in the direction of the garage. "Think Preston might have killed Royce? Outta jealousy?"

"It's certainly possible."

The garage wasn't a very big place, but it was a popular one. There were cars everywhere—cars that were about to be worked on, cars that were ready to be picked up, and cars belonging to the mechanics who worked there.

"You ain't got no car," said Wanda as they approached the garage.

"No. Red made sure of that years ago."

"Then what's yer excuse for bein' here?" asked Wanda.

"I'm campaigning," said Myrtle simply. "I'm asking for Preston's vote. You're here as a member of my campaign staff."

Wanda smiled a little to herself at the thought of being on someone's campaign staff.

Myrtle spotted Preston outside the garage looking at a car and waved. He raised his hand and immediately started coming over. Myrtle had to admit she wasn't exactly sure what Cindy had found appealing in Royce, especially compared to Preston. You could still see how Preston Cook had been a football star back in the day. He was still muscular, strong, and athletic looking. He'd been the high school's quarterback and had even gotten picked for a college team. At the time, though, Myrtle had wondered if Preston's academic performance would allow him to remain on a college team. Unfortunately, he hadn't been able to cut it as a student and had been forced to drop out. But he hadn't done poorly for himself—he'd started out as a mechanic at this garage and had ended up owning it. Still, though, Myrtle had always felt Preston had a lingering air of regret about him. As if he were living a life that he hadn't quite planned on.

"Miss Myrtle," said Preston, respectfully taking his baseball cap off as he walked up. "It's very good to see you."

Myrtle introduced Wanda and then said, "It's been a long time. How have you been?"

"Oh, pretty good, pretty good. You know how it is, Miss Myrtle. I don't have any complaints. Like I said, it sure is good to see you. I was just thinking about you the other day, as a matter of fact. You were such a good teacher and I still remember stuff you taught me. I feel like I write out decent invoices for customers because of your help."

Myrtle beamed at him. Preston's cell phone rang and he said, "Please excuse me for a second."

He put his cap back on his head so he could find his phone. He was fumbling with some of the aforementioned invoices, so Myrtle held out her hand for them. He thrust the papers gratefully at her as he spoke on the phone to a customer calling to check on his vehicle. Myrtle glanced over the invoices and sighed. There were plenty of errors on them. She hated to think they'd be even worse if Preston hadn't had her for high school English.

He quickly got off the phone and gave her a smile as he took back the papers. "Sorry about that. Now what can I do for you two ladies today? Miss Myrtle, I was thinking that you didn't have a car anymore. Is it Wanda who's having the car issues?"

Myrtle shook her head. "Actually, we're here on a completely different matter. I'm running for the vacant town council seat and Wanda is on my campaign staff."

Preston scratched his head. "Well, my goodness," he murmured. Apparently, if he'd been hazarding guesses as to why Myrtle was there, his imagination had failed him.

"Did you know I was running?" asked Myrtle.

"No ma'am. Sorry about that—I don't really follow politics."

"Did you know Royce Rollins was running against me?"

Preston shook his head slowly. "Nope. No, like I said, I just don't follow that kind of stuff. Maybe I should."

"You're registered to vote, though?" Myrtle's eyes narrowed as if she were preparing to launch into a lecture if there was a negative reply.

Preston latched onto this eagerly. "I sure am. You'll have my vote, Miss Myrtle. I have no doubt you could run this town. You sure ran a classroom like clockwork." He paused again and said, "You mentioned Royce. I think it was one of my customers who told me he'd passed."

"He surely did. Last night."

Preston shook his head. "That's awful. Must have been real unexpected. Last night was such a mess, wasn't it? I was here at the shop and drove right home to Cindy . . . didn't even stop at the store to pick up the milk she wanted. I managed to get home right before the rain started. Raining cats and dogs, it was."

"How is Cindy doing, by the way? It's been such a long time since I've seen her. She was always such an excellent student of mine."

Preston laughed ruefully, "Better than I was, for sure. She's okay." But there was a guarded look on his face now that hadn't been there before. It made Myrtle wonder if maybe Cindy *was* fine, but Cindy and Preston's relationship wasn't.

"Well, I am so sorry about Royce. My sympathies to you."

Preston looked a little taken aback and Myrtle continued, "But you two were always so friendly in high school, weren't you? It must be terrible to lose a friend, especially at your age. It must be such a shock."

Preston looked away. "We did know each other in high school, Miss Myrtle, but we were never very close. I really didn't know Royce at all." The last was said with a hint of bitterness. Then he slowly said, "You know, I hear things at the garage. The guys gossip between themselves and the customers come in with all kinds of stories, too. Lots of gossipy stuff going on there. I wouldn't be at all surprised if Scotty, Royce's son, had done him in."

"What makes you say that?" Myrtle's eyes narrowed again.

Preston shrugged and looked uncomfortable. "I don't know. I've heard that he was real hard on the kid. I guess he's not much of a kid now—early twenties? Anyway, he let Scotty live there, but never gave him a dime. Acted like he was just a freeloader. Maybe his son got tired of asking for money and being turned down."

"You think he might have killed Royce to get his hands on some inheritance money?" asked Myrtle.

"I guess it's possible, isn't it? I mean, it seems to me that he needed to do more for his son. Royce owned his own business, same as I do. If I had a son, I'd have him over here at the garage and teach him the business inside-out. The office, the shop. How to repair cars, how to run a business. The works. But Royce never had Scotty over there . . . at least, from what I heard from other people. To me, that was him doing a real disservice to his son."

One of the mechanics called out to Preston and he gave Myrtle and Wanda a regretful look. "Sorry, I guess I better go. You'll have my vote, Miss Myrtle, don't worry about that."

As he quickly headed back to the garage, Wanda croaked, "He's lying."

"Lying about what?" asked Myrtle.

Wanda shrugged, looking unhappy. "The sight don't—"

"I know, I know. The sight doesn't work that way. It seems to me that the sight is very picky about how it operates." Myrtle sighed. "Well, I know he's lying about one thing, anyway. That man did *not* pay enough attention in English class. His invoices were a real mess."

"What're we doin' the rest of the day?" asked Wanda.

"Hm. Good question. We could go harass Miles—that's always fun. We could make him watch *Tomorrow's Promise* with us. Or we could spend some time planning the fundraiser we're holding soon."

Wanda raised her eyebrows. "With them gnomes?"

"Sure. We'll pull it together pretty quickly. After all, my campaign isn't going to run for very long. It's not the kind of fundraiser that's going to take a lot of work. I'll just stick a sign in the yard that says 'take your picture with a gnome! $5 fundraiser!' Something like that." Myrtle snapped her fingers. "To really get attention, I could put *another* sign out that says 'honk if you like gnomes.' Then people will hear the honking and come around to see what's going on."

Wanda's eyes crinkled up. Myrtle was going to create quite a lively disturbance on Magnolia Lane.

Myrtle frowned. "Wait. What day is it?"

Wanda, who had never been tasked with keeping up with the days of the week, looked bemused.

"Uh-oh. It's garden club day. Ugh. I totally forgot about it." Myrtle made a face.

"Who's hostin' it?"

Myrtle brightened a little. "Actually, it's Tippy's day to host. What's more, she's going to have a speaker there so it shouldn't be as awful as it sometimes can be. Would you like to go? I know you enjoy growing things."

Wanda still did. Which was why Miles had taken her back home a couple of times since her stay with Myrtle—so that she could water the little living things she had in her house and out in her small garden.

Wanda nodded, eyes shining.

"Then let's get ready. We should probably wear our nicer clothes since we have the speaker and everything. Let's hope Erma isn't there. I'm surely *not* in the mood to be dealing with Erma's nonsense today."

Wanda grated in her croaky voice, "You know yer in a bit of a pickle, don't ya?"

"Am I? Over what?"

Wanda continued, "Yer competition jest died. An' now, if you drop out, Erma will be elected."

Myrtle stopped. "Oh no. No. I've been so caught up in thinking about who killed Royce that I didn't consider the consequences for the election. Well, there's only one thing to do. I'll have to persuade someone else to run."

"Ain't the deadline over?"

"The deadline *was* over. But now, one of the candidates isn't on the ballot anymore. I'm pretty sure I can get the town clerk to overlook a small technicality." Myrtle pressed her lips together grimly, thinking about the town clerk and how she was going to be forced to be flexible.

Myrtle and Wanda got ready for garden club and set off. Wanda borrowed one of Myrtle's small reporter notebooks and a pencil so she could take notes. Myrtle wasn't at all sure exactly what sort of notes Wanda was going to be able to take, considering she could barely read and write. She supposed there was going to be a lot of phonetic renditions of words, but however Wanda was able to make it work was good enough for Myrtle.

Tippy's house was a white-columned estate with well-manicured lawns and an interior full of expensive antiques. Myrtle looked thoughtfully at it as she and Wanda walked up. "I'm thinking Tippy might be just the person to help spread the word about our fundraiser."

"Thought you was gonna say she might be jest the person to go on the ballot," murmured Wanda.

Myrtle blinked at Wanda. "Do you think so?"

Wanda shrugged. "She likes to be involved. She's organized. She knows everybody."

Myrtle thought about this for a moment. "You're right. She might be the perfect candidate. Plus, her husband was political. Maybe some of it rubbed off on Tippy."

"Then do you need this money-raisin' thing?" asked Wanda. Her tone implied it was superfluous.

"Of course I do! It will be fun for the children. It will raise money for the charity I end up donating it to. And it will drive Red batty."

Wanda smiled.

Tippy, always the gracious hostess, met them at the door. She saw Wanda, dressed in her finest, and said, "Wanda! It's so very good to see you. I don't think I've seen you at garden club since you were at the last lecture we had. How's your gardening going?"

Wanda looked a bit guilty, knowing it had been neglected since she'd started staying with Myrtle. "It's okay. Could be better."

"Well, *all* of ours could be better, my dear. That's why we're here, isn't it? We get to listen to the experts tell us how to make magic in our yards! Come on in and let me make sure you know people here."

Myrtle watched in frustration as Tippy, elegant in a pale blush silk top and white slacks, swept away with Wanda in tow. Wanda looked behind her and gave Myrtle an eloquent helpless shrug of her thin shoulder.

"Did you bring Miles with you?" asked a breathless voice. Myrtle turned around to see another elderly member of garden club.

Miles was always quite the draw at either book club or garden club. He didn't belong to garden club, but Myrtle sometimes dragged him along as her guest. Or, as Miles considered it, her hostage.

"No, not this time. He was being rather antisocial today. I did bring Wanda, though."

The old woman's eyes lit up. "Did you, now?" She fidgeted, apparently trying to figure out how to gracefully disengage from the conversation with Myrtle and find Wanda. She likely wanted to pump her for information on whether she'd win at bingo the next week. It was all very vexing.

"You're dismissed," said Myrtle coolly, as if back in the classroom again.

The little old woman gratefully scuttled away.

There was a chuckle from behind her and Myrtle turned to see her friend Mercedes smiling at the exchange. Mercedes was, like Myrtle, another cane-wielder and had a good sense of humor. She was also a former teacher and was one of the ladies Myrtle gravitated toward during the sometimes-interminable garden club meetings, although she hadn't been at the one several days ago.

"You dispatched her really well, Myrtle," she said with a smile.

"Well, it takes practice. How are you doing, Mercedes?"

The other woman said, "From what I've heard, not as well as you are. Did I understand correctly that you're running for town council?"

Myrtle straightened just a little bit. Although she was eager to persuade Tippy to run for the seat, she might just miss having people admire her for being an octogenarian candidate for office. "You certainly did. I'm having a fundraiser soon, as a matter of fact, at my house." She tilted her head to one side. "As I recall, you taught Royce too, didn't you?"

Mercedes looked sad. "I did. I was sorry to hear the news about him." She blinked. "I just realized he must have been running against you."

Myrtle nodded. "Indeed he was. I believe Red has cleared me as a suspect, though. He better have, anyway. What did you think of him—Royce, I mean? I was wondering if you'd had the same impression of him as I did."

Mercedes said, "I had lots of impressions of him and few of them were good, I'm sad to say. Of course, I still feel terrible that such a young person with so much promise should be struck down like that."

Myrtle smiled a little. It was only very elderly people like Mercedes and herself that would think of a middle-aged person like Royce as a young person. Age was definitely relative.

"I was his neighbor for a while, too, you see. Until he grew wealthy and moved away to that huge home he left for." Mercedes put her hand over her mouth and glanced around, looking to make sure Tippy wasn't around. "I nearly forgot I *am* in a huge home. Anyway, I didn't think Royce was much of a neighbor." She gave Myrtle a thoughtful look. "Are you just generally interested in Royce's death, or are you interested as a reporter?"

"An investigative journalist," said Myrtle, puffing up again.

"Goodness but you do wear a lot of hats, Myrtle. Town council candidate *and* investigative reporter? I don't know how you do it all. Anyway, I was just going to add that you should speak with John DeMeo while you're here at garden club. He was talking to me when I saw him in the store yesterday about all this." Mercedes leaned on her cane and shook her head over the 'all this.'

"Royce's death, you mean?"

Mercedes nodded. "But more about Preston Cook." She glanced over near the refreshments table that Tippy had set out. "John is over there."

"Thanks," said Myrtle warmly, setting out to corner John as someone else came up to speak with Mercedes.

John was chatting with another gentleman as they were adding some of Tippy's fancy finger foods. Myrtle spotted stuffed mushrooms, prosciutto-wrapped cheeses, deviled eggs, and bite-sized quiches among loads of fresh fruits. Tippy had a way of making everyone else feel insecure about hosting book club or garden club.

The man John was speaking to quickly left, upon seeing the look of disapproval on Myrtle's face and perhaps thinking he might be the cause of it. John gave Myrtle a smile and she beamed back at him.

"Glad to see you today, Myrtle," said John. "You've missed a few of the last meetings, I noticed."

Myrtle preened. It was nice for someone to notice she hadn't been there. "Yes, I've been rather busy. Now I'm even busier."

"I saw you were running for local office," said John.

Myrtle nodded. "Yes. As a matter of fact, that's what I wanted to speak with you about. I feel terrible about Royce and what happened to him after our debate. I heard you might have some information about Preston Cook."

John raised his eyebrows. "Are you trying to track down Royce's killer?"

"Is it Preston Cook?" asked Myrtle.

John clearly did not want any part of tagging Preston as a murderer. He fumbled with his plate but quickly caught better hold of it before it tumbled to Tippy's pristine rug. John looked around them to make sure no one was listening in. Everyone, however, was surrounding Wanda. Wanda looked over at Myrtle and gave her a conspiratorial wink.

John cautiously said, "Myrtle, I have no idea. I don't want to point the finger at someone who had nothing to do with this."

"Which is very honorable of you. I wouldn't want you to do that anyway because it wouldn't be in the least helpful. What *would* be helpful is for you to just tell me what happened."

"It won't go into the newspaper?"

Myrtle said, "Certainly not. We don't print hearsay in the *Bradley Bugle*. That would be a poor business practice."

John nodded. "All right. The night of the debate, I was at Preston's garage. I'd brought my car in to get an oil change and tire rotation. It was busy there—lots of people were there picking up their vehicles. The woman before me left and she was wearing a large 'vote for Royce' button and was heading to the debate."

"Clearly a woman with poor taste." Myrtle pursed her lips.

"Exactly. Anyway, it really set Preston off. He was totally distracted and started talking trash about Royce. He seemed like he needed to unload."

"And you were kind enough to let him do it," said Myrtle.

"Actually, I really just wanted to get my car back and head home. The weather looked very threatening. You remember, I'm sure. But Preston was muttering about Royce. Said he was going to head over to the debate and interrupt it. He was going to fill everyone in on Royce's 'immoral activities' and 'not being a faithful husband to Jenny.'"

Myrtle raised her eyebrows. So Foley had been right. Cindy Cook *had* been involved with Royce. What was more, Preston had clearly found out about it. "What happened, I wonder? Preston never showed up at the debate."

John said, "Well, once I'd paid up and gotten the keys to my car back, Foley Hardy came in. From what I could tell before I left, he and Preston were starting to get into it over a transmission issue. Foley was asking for some sort of payment plan and for Preston to go ahead and fix it. But Preston was standing firm and saying that it was too expensive of a job for his shop to absorb the cost at the front end. That's when I left."

"So Foley held him up," said Myrtle quietly. "Perhaps for a long time. Maybe, by the time Preston finally made it to the debate, it was over." Preston, still wanting to fight, might have come across Royce on the staircase. She looked at John who was looking uneasy about what he'd said about Preston. "You've been very helpful. I'll let you eat now before the speaker starts."

Myrtle saw that, for an instant, Tippy was actually free from conversations. So she motioned her over.

# Chapter Thirteen

Tippy sailed over, glancing at Myrtle with concern. "Is everything all right? You're feeling all right? You're not eating any of the food." Tippy frowned thoughtfully at her carefully-arranged buffet of hors d'oeuvres as though analyzing whether something might be wrong with them.

"Everything is *not* fine," said Myrtle firmly. "We're facing a crisis in this town. I think you might be the only person to stop it."

Now Tippy looked alarmed. And somewhat worried, as if Myrtle might have suffered a small stroke when she entered Tippy's gracious home. "Whatever do you mean, Myrtle?"

"I mean that Royce Rollins is now dead, which clearly eliminates him from winning the town council seat. I've decided that perhaps the political life isn't for me." Myrtle decided not to say that she'd only entered the race to stir things up and scold the people who were in office. "But the problem is, if I drop out, the only candidate remaining is Erma."

They both looked across the room at Erma who was currently giving her braying laugh at something Erma herself had said to her companion.

"I see the predicament." Tippy pressed her lips together. "So you want me to persuade Benton to step into the race."

Myrtle scowled at this. She surely did *not* want Benton Chambers, Tippy's esteemed husband, to be on the ballot. She didn't think very much of him and his numerous affairs. Besides, he'd been a local politician for ages and nothing had improved. "Absolutely not. I want *you*, Tippy, to run."

Now Tippy really did look as if she thought Myrtle had suffered a small stroke. "Me? Why on earth would you want me to be on the town council, Myrtle?"

They were running out of time. The speaker was being herded to the small lectern by one of the officers of garden club. To Myrtle, Tippy was being deliberately obtuse. She snapped, "Because you're right for the job! You won't broker any foolishness on the town council. You'll make improvements. You're incredibly organized. You know everyone in this town. You'd be a *natural*, Tippy. Besides, I think it's your civic duty."

Myrtle knew that was the key that would end up making Tippy run. If there was one thing she had in spades, it was civic duty.

Tippy straightened a little. She already had excellent posture, so this straightening seemed to stretch her out to impossible heights.

Suddenly, Tippy and Myrtle were both clutched by a gasping woman. Myrtle turned to see Blanche Clark there. Blanche was, as usual, fashionably attired and beautifully made-up. "I just overheard what y'all were talking about. I'm just *so* excited. Why didn't I ever think about this before? Tippy, you'll make the perfect candidate." She paused, giving Myrtle an apologetic look. "Not that you weren't the perfect candidate, Myrtle."

Myrtle shrugged. "I was simply trying to restore peace and some order to the craziness of town council. And then there was a murder there. But I do believe Tippy can get everyone over there behaving themselves again. As a matter of fact, Tippy, if you want to go ahead and announce and get your paperwork signed, I can have my gnome fundraiser be for *your* campaign."

Tippy froze and looked across at Blanche. Apparently, the thought of a gnome fundraiser for her benefit was taking things just a little far. "I would have to discuss this with Benton first, of course. It will take some time to fill out the paperwork."

"You'll be amazed at how little time that can take," said Myrtle.

"So I think your fundraiser should be for your *own* campaign right now, Myrtle, thanks."

"All right. That money will be going to charity eventually, then. As long as you're really running. Otherwise, I suppose I have no alternative but to stay in the race. We have a lot to lose, otherwise."

Tippy and Myrtle turned as another braying laugh emitted from Erma. Blanche said, "Don't worry, Myrtle. I'll remind Tippy how great she'll be as a commissioner."

The speaker was better than Myrtle had anticipated, and she even found herself jotting down a few notes that would help with her tomato patch. Wanda, she saw, was laboriously trying to note everything the man said. But a few minutes in, Myrtle remembered that her phone had a voice recording feature on it that she sometimes used when doing interviews for the paper.

She showed Wanda that she was taping it and then Wanda relaxed and listened happily for the rest of the talk.

After garden club wrapped up, Myrtle noticed Wanda was looking very tired. She frowned. She *had* dragged Wanda all over town and on foot, at that. Myrtle still did have plans for her day. She thought she might make that casserole for Jenny, Royce's widow. But she doubted Wanda would make it to the grocery store. Then there was the fundraiser to plan.

"Are you doing all right, Wanda?" asked Myrtle, looking solicitously at her as they left Tippy's stately home.

"Jest real tired."

Myrtle frowned again. "I did have you walk all over town. Were those garden club women making you give them fortunes?"

"Not *fortunes*, really, but some tips." Wanda shrugged.

"But the kind of tips that only you can provide." Myrtle tightened her lips. People seemed to always ask a lot of Wanda. "I know you find that very draining. What would *you* like to do for the rest of the day?"

"What do you need doin'?" asked Wanda.

"No, no. This isn't about my stuff now. The rest of your day is yours to do with what you'd like."

Wanda considered this. After a while, Wanda said, "Reckon I'd like to listen to the garden club talk on yer phone. An' mebbe play Solitaire. Would be nice if the cat was with me, too."

Myrtle saw how happy Wanda looked at this very simple prospect. "Here are my keys and my phone. Just let yourself in and make yourself comfortable. I'm going to go get a few ingredients for the food I'm making for Jenny Rollins."

Wanda tilted her head doubtfully. "Ain't you gonna need help with carryin' the food?" She looked pointedly at Myrtle's cane.

"Not a bit. I'm only going to get one small bag, which I can dangle from my left arm. I'll see you soon, don't worry."

Wanda set off slowly toward Myrtle's house as Myrtle strode decisively for the Piggly Wiggly grocery store.

Myrtle noticed with irritation that everyone in town seemed to have the same idea at the same time and the store was quite crowded. She picked up a plastic shopping basket to remind herself that she didn't need to get too many items or she'd have to call Miles or even Red to drive her back home with them. She started mulling over the ingredients for her Chicken Spectacular recipe. Canned chicken . . . of that she was quite confident. Cream of whatever soup. The other ingredients were a little harder to remember. Was it canned green beans? Canned asparagus? Pimentos?

While she was considering the vagaries of the recipe, someone softly said her name behind her. She turned and saw Jenny Rollins there.

"Miss Myrtle," said Jenny with a smile. "I thought that was you."

Jenny was still a very beautiful woman. In fact, Myrtle considered that Royce had not had very good taste in straying from her. She was very tall, just as tall as Myrtle was. But where Myrtle was solidly constructed, Jenny was willowy with delicate features and high cheekbones. She had blonde hair cut short, which enhanced her angular face. Now she looked rather pale and drawn, almost certainly from the recent events and the loss of her husband.

"Jenny! Goodness. Here I am shopping for ingredients to make you a casserole. I am just so sorry about Royce's death. What a terrible shock that was for all of us, especially for you."

Jenny gave a forced smile and looked askance at the contents of Myrtle's shopping basket. She had put all the possible variations of ingredients in there.

"Myrtle," said Jenny in her cultured voice, "that is so very kind of you."

Myrtle straightened a bit, pleased. "It's the least I can do, Jenny. I just feel awful about poor Royce. He was a very worthy challenger for the town council seat."

Jenny continued, "Well, I can't tell you how much I appreciate it. But I simply can't allow you to make me food and tote all that home. Some ladies from the church came by just a little while ago and I'm completely inundated with food. I put most of it in the freezer. I don't think Scotty or I will ever have to make food again." She said the last with a chuckle.

Myrtle was doubtful. "The church ladies do tend to swarm. But if you're here at the store, don't you still need things?"

Jenny swiftly answered, "Only some paper towels. That's all I've popped in for. Again, it's so sweet of you, but I can't let you take the trouble."

Jenny seemed quite firm on this point, so Myrtle put the various vegetables back on the shelf in front of her.

"How are you doing?" asked Myrtle with concern. Because the truth was, Jenny didn't look all that well.

She gave a short laugh. "Oh, I'm hanging in there. There's nothing else to do, is there? I do need paper towels, but another reason I'm here is simply to get out of the house. I don't think I can stand another minute in there right now. Too many memories."

"At least you have Scotty there with you," said Myrtle warmly. "That must be a great comfort to you."

Jenny gave a rueful sigh. "Well, I have him temporarily. But the truth of the matter is that I thought it was time for him to spread his wings. It's what Scotty's been wanting to do for such a long while. Royce was a good father, but a stern one. I've decided to give Scotty a loan and help him go out on his own. It was something of a split-second decision for me, which isn't what I usually do. But when Scotty feels emotional about anything, he hides it. Buries it. And then plays very loud music as therapy."

Myrtle nodded. "I have the feeling that your own way of dealing with grief doesn't involve loud music?"

"I could use some quiet time on my own," admitted Jenny. "So right now there are a bunch of boxes in my house as Scotty gets his things together. He does have a friend he's going to live with, so he'll have a roommate. That's a good thing because he's never lived on his own before. When he was at college he was in a dorm, which is very different."

Myrtle said, "That's probably just as good for Scotty as it is for you."

"Royce just didn't want to fund it," said Jenny with a sigh. "We had a good relationship but naturally we didn't agree with each other on everything."

Her voice was leaden with grief. Myrtle just nodded again and waited for Jenny to continue if she wanted to. And she did.

"I simply can't imagine anyone doing this. I've been mulling it all over in my head until I feel like my head is going to burst. It hasn't helped with the constant headache I've had, either. One of the reasons I wanted to say hi was to ask if anything happened at the debate. If you noticed anything or anybody acting as if they had ill-will toward Royce."

Myrtle shifted as Jenny watched her intently. "Well, I wouldn't say I witnessed any *ill-will*. It was a lively debate, of course. Royce was rather scrappy."

Jenny shook her head. "Maybe not so much the debate itself, but before it? Or afterward?"

Myrtle had been preoccupied with getting to the elevator without anyone snickering at her. Red had been fairly distracting, as well. She hadn't wanted to speak with Erma, despite standing up for her during the debate. She said, "I'm afraid I had other things on my mind and didn't stay very long. The weather was about to change, too, and we wanted to get back to our homes. But I didn't notice Royce arguing with anyone or anybody being really obstreperous."

Jenny looked disappointed.

Myrtle asked, "I did understand that Bonner Lang and your husband had something of a challenging relationship."

Jenny waved her hand dismissively. "Oh, that's just business. Nothing personal."

Myrtle tilted her head to one side. It was interesting that Jenny seemed to suppose Royce's death had personal motives.

"I'd imagine that business-related issues that tied into financial income might well be a motive," said Myrtle.

Jenny gave a languid shrug. "Money is always supposed to be the key to everything, isn't it? I'm just not sure about it in this case. After all, Bonner was the one who kept Royce from getting the lucrative contract. Shouldn't Royce have murdered Bonner, instead of the other way around?"

"That would have made the most sense, but then I wondered if one of the reasons Royce was running for office to begin with was to stymie Bonner on the council. To vote against projects or proposals that Bonner was interested in."

Jenny had a small smile on her face. "That does sound possible, Miss Myrtle. Royce did sometimes play hardball that way. I could see him being a little vengeful sometimes."

Myrtle asked curiously, "Is there someone else you think could have been involved? You seemed to think it wasn't a business-related motive at all . . . does that mean you think the motive was more personal?"

Jenny stiffened and her face grew mask-like. "I really have no idea, Miss Myrtle, just like I said." She swiftly changed topics. "I did want to ask what you intended to do about running for office. Are you staying in? Is it you and Erma who are campaigning for the empty seat now?"

Myrtle winced a little at the mention of Erma. "Yes, well, I'm in for now. In fact, I'm going to have a fundraiser soon. A photo opportunity for families with my gnomes."

Jenny gave a startled laugh. "Well, that will be very interesting, Myrtle. I hope you have a good turnout."

"But to answer your question, I'm hoping that Tippy Chambers will be entering the race for the seat. I'm very fond of Tippy and think she would make a wonderful commissioner. If she does enter, I'd have no problem dropping out."

Jenny said, "Oh good. Tippy is always so organized and involved. I can't think why she hasn't been in local politics before now."

"Apparently, she thought it was the sole provenance of her husband, Benton. But now she's at least considering it. She said she'd run it by Benton and see what his thoughts are." Myrtle looked at Jenny consideringly. "You've never thought about running for office?"

Jenny smiled. "No. Never. I don't think I'd enjoy it at all. Royce was the one who liked being, as you said, scrappy. He was more of the ideas person."

"And you're the one who gets things done?" asked Myrtle lightly. "The power behind the throne?"

Jenny's smile turned a little stressed. "Well, there was no throne involved, was there? Let's just say we made a good team." She glanced at her watch. "Well, I've held you up for entirely too long, Miss Myrtle. It was so good to see you."

It was definitely a dismissal. Myrtle watched thoughtfully as Jenny headed toward the paper towel aisle.

# Chapter Fourteen

Since Jenny had effectively torpedoed Myrtle's plans to bring her food, she was now trying to piece together what she wanted to do next. She still needed to plan for the gnome fundraiser by making signs. Should she serve snacks? She decided to get a few bags of potato chips since there would likely be kids there. While she was at the store, she contemplated what she and Wanda should eat for supper. They'd eaten out a bit lately and Myrtle's pocketbook was feeling the pinch. But she did feel that they should perhaps eat vegetables and fruits. It was unfortunate, since produce was pretty much the most expensive thing at the store.

She bought a motley assortment of some of the least-expensive items in the produce department. This meant that her plastic basket held bananas, corn on the cob, carrots, and a couple of apples. Myrtle was fairly sure that she had hummus at home for the carrots. At least, she hoped so. The plastic basket was heavy enough as it was.

A couple of quiet days later, Royce's funeral was held. Myrtle donned her funeral outfit which was amazingly clean since she'd washed it after she'd worn it at the debate. She swore the garment managed to soil itself as she was frequently confounded by the way it would attract spills. Satisfied with her appearance, she and Wanda rode with Miles out to the cemetery for the graveside service.

The funeral was quite blustery. For a terrible moment, it looked as if the tent over the mourners might become airborne. The funeral director's face was even grimmer than usual.

The family insisted Myrtle sit down under the tent, regardless of its wild undulations. She'd protested, preferring to see the assembled group's reactions. But they wouldn't hear of it and ushered her to a seat. Myrtle looked grimly behind her. Miles, apparently too youthful to get preferential treatment, was uncomfortably standing about six feet away from Wanda, perhaps not wanting to fuel small-town gossip mills that they were some sort of couple. Wanda, her new, used clothes blowing in the wind around her emaciated frame, lent a sort of gothic feel to the proceedings.

The service was short and sweet, which was definitely to Myrtle's liking. There was a mournful-sounding soloist which made many of the gathered mourners surreptitiously dab at their eyes. Jenny, however, stayed granite-faced and pale, eyes trained ahead of her, hands folded in her lap. She was the picture of reserved calm. Scotty kept shifting uncomfortably in his seat and looking away as if wishing he were anywhere else. No one spoke aside from the rather dry minister who kept his comments brief.

Afterward, the minister mentioned that the assembled mourners had been invited to the Rollins home for the funeral reception. Everyone left for their cars and drove to the large home, parking on both sides of the residential street.

Myrtle glanced over at Wanda who was looking very calm in the backseat. "Are you sure you don't want Miles to drop you off by the house?"

"I wouldn't mind at all," said Miles with alacrity. He'd attended quite a few funerals lately and was feeling as if he'd already done his duty by this one.

Wanda shook her head. "I'm okay."

"We won't stay for long," said Myrtle. "There's one thing I'm sure there'll be plenty of and that's food. With Jenny so involved in the community and church, it's going to be quite a spread of delectable goodies."

And it was. There were all the usual Southern funeral dishes: fried chicken, potato salad, pimento cheese sandwiches with the crusts cut off, deviled eggs, corn pudding, green bean casserole, and more. But there was already a big line waiting to go through the buffet.

"Pooh," said Myrtle. "I suppose we should mingle for a little while until the line goes down."

Perhaps because it was a funeral reception, people were more willing to leave Wanda alone instead of pestering her for fortunes. But their eyes watched her curiously as she followed Myrtle and Miles to the back of the living room where Myrtle could watch people back.

Myrtle prodded Miles. "Look. Preston is trying to talk to Jenny."

"Looks like he's trying to argue, not talk," said Miles slowly.

And indeed, Preston was leaning forward earnestly trying to tell Jenny something—something it was clear that Jenny didn't want to hear. She finally gave him a cold look and abruptly turned away to speak with someone else.

"I wonder what that was about," said Miles.

"Maybe Preston was trying to tell Jenny that Royce wasn't worth her tears," said Myrtle, eyes narrowed thoughtfully. "Maybe he wanted to make sure she was aware that Royce was having an affair with Cindy."

"Whatever it was, it was obvious she didn't want to hear it. Or maybe, to believe it," said Miles.

Wanda watched the room gravely. Then she said in her raspy voice, "Should stop her."

Myrtle gave her a startled look. "Who? Jenny?"

Wanda shook her head. "Naw. Erma."

Myrtle redirected her attention to a different part of the room where Erma was loudly regaling everyone within earshot—which, considering Erma's volume, was everyone gathered there.

Myrtle grimaced. "Must I? I really don't want to be Erma's keeper."

"You stood up for her at the debate," pointed out Miles.

"Yes, I did. I think that's the end of it. She's a grown woman and she should be able to contain herself, especially at a funeral reception." But Myrtle did listen to hear what Erma was saying.

"So that's why I'm running for town council. Be sure to vote for me, haha!" She glanced down at her plate. "Wow, this rice dish is super-spicy. I have this issue with heartburn—it's even *worse* than heartburn . . . there's a special name for it, but I've forgotten. Anyway, going back to town council. You know I was there the night Royce died. Well, I left, of course, after the debate but Royce was still there. I had to go back to town hall because I'd forgotten something. The weather was awful! I could barely even see! But as soon as I drove up to the building, I got this really strange feeling. It was spooky. The hair on the back of my neck stood up on end. I knew something terrible was happening."

Erma's tone was that of someone entertaining an audience—like someone telling a ghost story. Myrtle rolled her eyes at Miles and Wanda. "Utterly ridiculous," she muttered.

"When I went back, I saw something." Erma glanced around to make sure she had everyone's attention. And she did. A smug look crossed her features. "I can't say anything more about that. I wish I could disclose what I saw, but I must speak with Red first."

The faces of everyone ranged from disbelief to hostility. They'd been denied the rest of their story. With some grumblings, most of them moved away to the buffet table for first helpings or seconds while Erma attempted to regale the remaining stragglers with more health-related atrocities.

As the last few people quickly made excuses and moved on, Myrtle called out to Erma and she obediently came over, grinning at Myrtle with her donkey-like face still looking smug from the tale she told.

Myrtle said sternly, "Erma, you're being very foolish. The last thing you need to do is to tell a group of people, one of whom may be a murderer, that you know important information about Royce's death."

Erma's face fell. "I didn't say anything, though. I said I was going to talk to Red."

"Precisely. If you *had* told everyone, then you wouldn't be in danger because the murderer wouldn't be able to kill twenty or thirty people. But because you didn't, someone might take it into their heads to eliminate you before you have the chance to talk about what you saw. If anything," said Myrtle, giving Erma a patently doubtful look.

"But I did see something!"

"Then go tell Red about it," said Myrtle. "He's here somewhere. It's the perfect time."

Erma lifted her chin stubbornly. "I will. After I eat."

"For further protection, you should tell Miles, Wanda, and me what you saw." Myrtle folded her hands in her lap in a waiting pose.

Erma shook her head. "Nope. I'm not going to say anything until I talk to Red. Like I said, I'm going to get something to eat now before all the food is gone." With that, she scurried over to the huge array of food, which was in no danger of running out.

"Complete and utter foolishness," said Myrtle, narrowing her eyes at Erma's back. "This is the kind of thing I deal with day in and day out."

"Try and put it out of your mind," said Miles. "We need to eat, too. This is our reward for being at this funeral, remember?"

"It's been a frightfully disappointing funeral from an information-gathering aspect. Let's wait a moment before we go to the buffet. I don't want to be behind Erma in line. Then we may end up sitting next to each other," said Myrtle with a shudder.

So they waited, stomachs growling, as Erma slowly made her way through the buffet line, heaping her plate so high that it looked as if food was going to be tumbling off it at any second.

"Oh, good. She's joined another group and is torturing them," said Myrtle. "Let's go."

They did and filled their plates up with some delicious food, which they quickly gobbled up. Then, much to Miles's satisfaction, they left shortly after eating, since there was no additional information to be had.

Miles took them back home and then Myrtle set out for a walk to clear her head.

When she got back home, she found a solemn Wanda sitting at her kitchen table. Instead of regular playing cards, she was holding her tarot cards. Pasha was looking very tense nearby.

Myrtle frowned at the grim look on Wanda's face. "What's happened? Or . . . what's going to happen?"

"Nothin' good," grated Wanda. She gave a shiver and Myrtle frowned even more severely. She found a blanket in the linen closet and draped it around Wanda's cadaverous shoulders.

"You've gotten yourself all wound up," said Myrtle. "If you don't have more information about the bad things that are going to happen, then let's get you doing something else."

Wanda looked sad. "Somethin' bad's gonna happen tonight. Feels like death."

"Not mine or yours, I hope," said Myrtle briskly.

Wanda shook her head.

"Then let's not fret over it. That's all you know?"

Wanda nodded miserably.

"Then we won't worry. We will just be alert. I don't sleep anyway, so I'm sure I can hear if something goes amiss. Now put those cards away and you and I will play hearts."

So they played cards and then they ate fruit and vegetables for supper. Myrtle made the signs she needed for the fundraiser the next day. Then Myrtle turned in while Wanda stayed up in the kitchen, playing solitaire and looking somber.

That night, despite what Myrtle told Wanda, she was more than alert. She was on edge. This meant that she tossed around in her bed for a while. Then she pulled her book out and tried to read. Finally, she gave up and deserted her bedroom for the kitchen. Sometimes a snack was good for sleeping, she told herself. However, the snack she chose was a sugary one, so perhaps not the best choice for falling asleep.

As she was biting into her second cookie, there was a bloodcurdling scream outside.

Myrtle bolted outside in her robe and slippers, heading in the direction of the scream, thumping with her cane as she hurried down her front walk. Wanda, rubbing her eyes, hurried after her, a blanket wrapped around her pajamas.

"Who is it?" grated Wanda.

"I'd know that scream anywhere," said Myrtle grimly. "That was Erma."

The scream continued on and on as lights popped on in the houses around them, Red's front door flew open and he charged out, looking very groggy.

"What is it? What's going on? Are you okay, Mama?" he yelled across the street at them.

"It's not me. It's Erma." Myrtle muttered to Wanda, "As if I would scream like that."

Miles came bolting out of his house, a navy robe over his plaid pajamas. Myrtle gestured him over.

"Erma?" he asked as he strode over, watching as Red dashed over to Erma's backyard where the screams were continuing.

"Yes. But surely she can't be that badly off and still be making that much racket," said Myrtle.

"Shouldn't we stay back? Let Red handle it?" asked Miles as Myrtle kept walking toward Erma's backyard.

"Nonsense. Besides, I already know what happened."

"What? How do you know?" asked Miles.

"Death," grated Wanda.

"Wanda knew before we turned in. Got the chills from it."

Red appeared again as they stood in Erma's side-yard. He was moving Erma with determination from her backyard toward Myrtle. "Mama," he said loudly over the continued screaming. "Can you take Erma to your house?"

For the first time ever, Myrtle was happy to invite Erma over. "Yes." She turned to Erma and said forcefully in her very best teacher voice, "*Stop* it, Erma. *Now*."

Erma took a gasping breath and stared at Myrtle.

"We're going to go to my house to have milk and cookies," Myrtle said firmly.

"Store-bought cookies?" asked Erma hopefully.

Miles hid a smile.

"Yes, yes, store-bought cookies. Come along. Everyone is gaping at us and lollygagging."

Sure enough, neighbors up and down the street were watching Erma being escorted next door to Myrtle's house and Red was now making a phone call, presumably to the state police. Since, as Wanda had promised, someone was certainly dead.

# Chapter Fifteen

They walked into Erma's house and Wanda took the blanket off and wrapped it around Erma's shoulders since Erma was shaking uncontrollably. Myrtle dumped the remaining cookies onto a plate and poured Erma a glass of milk.

Miles cleared his throat. "Perhaps something a little stronger might be good, as well. Something more medicinal."

Myrtle said, "I'll find the sherry."

A moment later, Erma was consuming an odd mix of sherry, milk, and cookies. Her color, such as it was, was starting to return so she wasn't ghostly white anymore but merely her usual, pale self.

Erma, true to form, was starting to realize she had an audience. And a spotlight. She sat a bit straighter and the light returned to her eyes.

Seeing this, Myrtle asked, "Now Erma, if it's not too upsetting, can you tell us what happened? I'm assuming you weren't screaming because of some horrid health-related malady?"

Erma shook her head. "No. Although I did have quite an upset stomach directly after the funeral reception. Something didn't agree with me. Maybe it was the fried chicken. Or maybe the deviled eggs. But my intestines—"

"That's quite enough talk of intestines. *What happened?*"

Erma swallowed and looked sadly down at her plate of cookies. "I heard a noise outside. I haven't been sleeping very well since Royce's death. I started wondering if someone was planning on murdering *all* the candidates for the town council spot!" She looked wildly around at Myrtle, Miles, and Wanda. "That puts you in danger, too, Myrtle."

Myrtle did not seem in the least perturbed at being in this sort of danger. "I hardly think that was the motive for Royce's murder, Erma. But please, continue." Especially since Red would most likely be there in the next minute or so.

Erma took a deep breath. "I picked up a frying pan as a weapon and I carefully looked out my back window. It was the backyard that the noises were coming from. I saw something out there, but you know how dark it was. I couldn't tell what it was. I opened the door and tiptoed out and it was *Preston*! He was dead in my yard!"

The last couple of sentences were said in a shrieking tone that made Myrtle fear the worst for the continuation of Erma's previous screaming. She refilled Erma's sherry and said, "Have some, Erma."

Erma obeyed, picking up the tiny sherry glass with a trembling hand.

Myrtle, Miles, and Wanda looked at each other in puzzlement. Why had Preston been in Erma's yard? How had he died there?

As Myrtle thought, Red came back, shoving the door open and looking at the gathered group in the kitchen with his hands on his hips. He relaxed a little when he saw the rather domestic scene in front of him, with no screaming involved.

He pulled up a chair and gave Erma a concerned look. "Are you doing all right?"

Erma asked meekly, "You mean in general, with all my health conditions? Or just specific to what happened a few minutes ago?"

Red clearly had no desire to be relegated with a dozen of Erma's most-grotesque medical issues. "Just in regard to what took place tonight."

Erma nodded.

Myrtle said, "Before you start asking her questions, Red, I think it's fair if you give us a little information. Erma will feel a lot better if she knows more about what happened and maybe she'll make a bit more sense."

Miles smiled at the implication that Erma hadn't been making enough sense to satisfy Myrtle.

Red rubbed his eyes. "Okay. Erma, I guess you know who was out in your yard."

Erma nodded again, this time bobbing her head up and down so wildly Myrtle thought her eyeballs might be rattling around in her head. "Preston Cook!"

"All right. I can confirm that he is dead. Lieutenant Perkins, who has been staying locally while investigating Royce's death, is at the scene ensuring it stays undisturbed."

"I'm assuming it wasn't a natural death," said Myrtle. "That Preston didn't, for some bizarre reason, wander into Erma's yard and have a heart attack there."

Red shook his head. "I'm afraid it was definitely murder."

Erma gave another shriek that made everyone jump. "Why? Why was he in my yard?"

Red said in a calm voice, "We're going to get to the bottom of this, I promise you. Do you have any information you can give me to help me get started? Did you have any interactions with Preston recently?"

"No. No! I barely know the man." She gasped. "You don't think he had any romantic notions about me? You don't think he was going to throw pebbles at my window or something?"

Red blinked at her. Then he said in a soothing voice, "No, I don't think that was it. I didn't see any pebbles in his hand. But I do wonder why he was in your yard."

Erma grabbed her throat, eyes wild. "I don't know! I really don't know!"

Myrtle noticed that Wanda had a knowing, tired look in her eyes. She bet that Wanda had some idea what he might have been doing there.

Red said gravely, "Okay, Erma, I think we're going to be able to let you back in your house, but you're going to need to put on a pair of booties to go through your yard to get in, just in case there's any evidence outside that we need to protect."

Erma nodded. "I'll do it."

"Just make sure you don't go outside." Red's voice was stern.

Erma shook her head. "I won't!"

Red led Erma away and Miles, Wanda, and Myrtle sat at the kitchen table, looking at each other.

"What on earth was that all about?" asked Miles.

Myrtle said, "I haven't the faintest idea, but I believe Wanda does."

Wanda nodded, sadly. "That funeral."

"Where Erma was running her mouth," said Myrtle knowingly.

Wanda said, "She was being too loud an' actin' like she knew stuff."

"That's Erma's normal behavior," said Myrtle with a weary sigh. "But she can't do that when there's a murderer out and about."

Miles rubbed his temples. "Wait. Maybe I'm still trying to wake up, but I don't totally understand what the two of you are saying. Are you saying that *Preston* was at Erma's house to kill her?"

"She said she had important info," drawled Wanda.

Miles said, "What's hard for me to understand is that anyone who knew Erma would think that she *had* any important information. Like Myrtle was saying: she's always acting like she has a vital piece of gossip that really isn't. Or that her medical complaints are so important that she has to share them with everybody else. Why would Preston believe her?"

"Desperation," said Myrtle coolly. "He probably also doesn't know Erma as well as we do. He might have thought she really *did* know something and thought she was going to expose him. So he crept up through her backyard to do away with her and eliminate the risk."

"And she killed him?" Miles was frowning. "Self-defense?"

Wanda shook her head. "Said she *found* a body."

"But was she likely to say she just killed someone?" asked Miles.

Myrtle said, "This is Erma we're talking about. You saw the state she was in. As much as she likes telling tall tales, there's no way she'd have the intellectual capacity to come up with a cover story. No, she'd have been blabbing to all of us that she hit him over the head with her frying pan because he was going to kill her." She frowned. "We need to find out if Erma actually *does* know something. That's the problem with Erma."

"There's only one?" asked Miles.

"Well, it's the biggest problem with Erma right now. We're so used to her being unhelpful that when she might actually *be* helpful, we're doubtful about it. Tomorrow morning we'll need to talk to her."

Wanda drawled, "Along with everybody else on the street."

"Oh, they've probably already gone back to bed," said Myrtle, waving a dismissive hand.

Miles got up and walked to Myrtle's living room window to peek out through the blinds. "Their lights are still on."

"Well, we have an advantage. We'll go *early*."

"How early?" asked Miles warily.

"Maybe in a couple of hours. Once the forensics people are done with the yard."

Miles said, "You do know it will be 4:30 a.m. in a couple of hours. You might well give Erma a heart attack if you arrive at that time, considering Preston was in her yard trying to kill her just a short while ago."

"As far as I'm aware, Erma has no heart conditions at all," said Myrtle breezily. "She really only complains about her skin and her intestines. Besides, how likely is she to go back to sleep, considering all the drama going on in her yard?"

Miles and Wanda looked at her and Myrtle snapped, "Okay, okay. I'll give her a phone call, how about that? That's less-scary than a doorbell ringing or a knock on the door."

"Good idea," said Wanda.

"Now, I'm assuming that we're *not* going to try to return to bed. Is that what you two are thinking? Because I don't believe I've ever been so wide-awake in my life," said Myrtle.

Wanda shrugged. "Don't feel real sleepy."

Miles sighed. "I suppose I might as well stay up at this point. Although it *is* the middle of the night."

Myrtle said, "Excellent! So it's a party. I'll pull out crackers and cheese and we'll watch our soap opera."

Miles flinched, as he usually did, when she applied the pronoun *our* to "soap opera".

Wanda looked hopeful and Myrtle added, "And then we'll play cards."

A couple of hours later of happy companionship, Myrtle looked at the clock. "I do believe it's time for me to make my phone call to Erma. I must get to her before everyone else on the street does."

"I think everyone else on the street has finally fallen back asleep," said Miles wryly.

"Nevertheless, it's time. We've got a busy day ahead, remember? We have to go out into the community! Speak to people.

Figure out what's happened to Preston and Royce. Plus, I really must bake Cindy a casserole."

Miles winced at the mention of the casserole.

Wanda drawled, "An' the fundraiser? Them gnomes?"

"Ah, yes. Well, that won't take very long, will it? I really should follow up with Tippy, too, and ensure that Benton isn't being ridiculous about her wanting to run for office." Myrtle pursed her lips, looking displeased at the thought of Benton being unreasonable.

"But it wasn't really Tippy who wanted to run, was it? Wasn't it more that you wanted her to run?" Miles gave her a reproving look.

Myrtle said briskly, "It's that Tippy is the perfect candidate. I won't have to worry about silly shenanigans going on during town council meetings if Tippy is there. She's a grown-up. People automatically behave themselves around her because she commands respect." She scowled. "Believe me, if Benton tries to talk her out of it, I will certainly be having words with him." Her expression boded ill for Benton if he tried to get in Myrtle's way.

She picked up the phone and dialed Erma's number. It rang once and then was picked up by a gasping Erma. "Hello? *Hello?*"

"Erma? It's Myrtle."

There was a gusty sigh of relief on the other end. "Oh, it's you. I thought Preston's killer might be after me. Myrtle, do you think I'm next?"

Myrtle said in a firm voice, "No, Erma, I don't. In fact, I think the real danger posed to you was from Preston. I have the feeling he wasn't in your backyard last night because he was planning a friendly visit. But now that he's gone, I'm thinking you're safe. But what I really wanted to know is what *you* know. What's the vital information you have that made Preston think he needed to permanently silence you?"

Erma howled on the other end. "I don't knooooow! I really don't, Myrtle!"

Myrtle scolded, "You must, Erma. You were saying at Royce's funeral that you had new insights into his death. What was it that you meant?"

Erma's voice was subdued now. "I don't think I really meant anything. I *thought* I might know something, but I really don't. I was at the scene of the murder. I went back for my medical alert bracelet thing. I was showing it to somebody at the debate and I must have set it down when I was speaking to them and forgot it. I thought maybe someone would still be in the town hall building—maybe the custodial staff would be there cleaning up. But the lights were all off and I knew I couldn't get inside."

"Did you see anyone leave? Did you see a car there? Was there anything that looked wrong or out of place?"

Erma wept. "I don't know! I really don't. I think I saw a car, but it was raining so hard that I couldn't really tell what it looked like. I was focused on trying to get inside the building so I wasn't paying that much attention."

Sadly, this all sounded very likely. As Myrtle had thought, Erma didn't know *anything*. But Preston had clearly thought she had and that led to his death. "Try to get some rest," said Myrtle. She paused. "It might be kind of noisy over at my house today. I'm having a fundraiser in a little while. It's a sort of impromptu thing."

Erma yawned on the other end. "I'll try to come by," she said sleepily.

"No! No, that's not necessary, Erma. You've had a long enough day already and it's barely started. I was simply explaining that there might be children and cars so you might want to put headphones on or earplugs or something."

"It's okay—I'll pop over. It's a fundraiser."

"Yes, Erma, but it's a fundraiser for an *opposing candidate*. It doesn't really make sense if you come over."

Myrtle listened, but didn't hear anything on the other end. "Erma?"

There was a loud, rattling snore on Erma's end and Myrtle hung up the phone.

"Nothing?" asked Miles.

Myrtle made a face. "Worse than nothing. She doesn't know anything *and* she's planning on making an appearance at my fundraiser." She looked at her watch. "Which perhaps I should set up for now."

"It's still dark outside," said Miles, looking somewhat appalled. "There's no point in putting everything out there now."

"It will hang over me until it's done," said Myrtle. She stood up and got her homemade signs.

"I'll help," croaked Wanda, standing up.

Miles reluctantly stood. "I will, too. I guess. Although I still think we could wait until it's a little later. At least until sunrise."

"Could you lift that folding table, Miles? Wanda, if you'll grab the snacks I picked up at the store. And I suppose we need some sort of box or something for everyone to put their donations in."

Miles wrestled the table to the driveway and pulled the legs out and stood it up. Wanda set the food out. Pasha, who had been hunting around the gnomes, watched them all curiously.

"Myrtle?" came a quiet call from the street as Myrtle was putting a sign in her yard.

Myrtle gave a short yelp of surprise and then peered into the darkness. Cindy Cook was standing there.

# Chapter Sixteen

Miles and Wanda froze.

Myrtle said, "Goodness, Cindy. Are you all right? What are you doing out here? Come inside. We have snacks. And... sherry."

Myrtle carefully picked her way around the gnomes and led the way into her house. Cindy was shivering and Myrtle picked up the blanket that had also given comfort to Wanda and Erma and threw it around Cindy's shoulders as she bustled her to the kitchen table.

Myrtle, Miles, and Wanda stared anxiously at Cindy, who did look quite pale and hollow-eyed. This likely, of course, was due to the fact that Cindy must have just recently found out that she had been widowed.

Miles said slowly, "Sherry, I think, Myrtle."

Myrtle pulled a wine glass out of the cabinet and hurriedly poured a full glass and shoved it at Cindy. She kept her fingers crossed that Cindy wasn't going to suddenly burst into tears. Myrtle always felt helpless when people did that around her and she didn't think Miles or Wanda were going to be much better.

Cindy took a long gulp from the glass and then coughed. She drained the glass as Myrtle blinked. If Myrtle had a glass of sherry, she usually nursed it until at least an hour had gone by. The good news was, however, that Cindy's cheeks were now stained with color.

"You heard," said Cindy.

"About Preston? Yes. Cindy, I'm so, so sorry."

Cindy nodded dully, looking down at the empty glass. Miles helpfully filled it up again and Cindy took another big gulp.

"I've lost everything now," she said simply. She glanced around at the three of them and suddenly seemed to realize where she was and what she was doing. "I'm sorry for horning in. Thanks for this. After Red told me, I just couldn't stay holed up in the house. I couldn't even call anybody because it was so early. So I just set out for a walk and then saw y'all outside." She frowned a little as if it occurred to her that *that* was rather odd, too—these three people setting up signs and tables in the dark.

"Red woke you up, I suppose," said Myrtle. "That must have been extremely disorienting right there."

Cindy nodded. "I'd been at home all night. I turned in early, so I did get some sleep."

Miles said, "Preston was home with you? When you turned in?"

"Yes. Well, he'd worked sort of late at the garage, but that's pretty common. He was home before I went to sleep, though. He knows I don't sleep really well when he's not there." She gave a bewildered shrug. "I guess he must have slipped out at some point. When Red told me where he was found, I couldn't believe it. Part of me wanted to just check all the rooms of the house and check the backyard. He'd been right *there*, with me. It's just hard for me to wrap my head around this."

Myrtle asked, "Do you have any idea what Preston was doing at Erma's house, Cindy?"

Cindy shook her head, looking baffled. "I have absolutely no idea. I mean, nobody really seeks Erma out, do they?"

But there was something about Cindy's expression that made Myrtle wonder if perhaps Cindy *did* have an idea what Preston might have been doing there. "Can you tell us anything about Preston's demeanor since Royce died?"

Cindy knitted her brows and Myrtle elaborated. "How has Preston seemed? Has he been acting differently?"

"Oh, yes. Yes. I was wondering if Preston might have known something that made him a target. Maybe he was investigating on his own?"

Myrtle thought this was highly unlikely. Perhaps some of this feeling crossed her features because Cindy said, "Yeah, you're probably right. Maybe he wasn't really investigating, but he did know something. He's been acting really tense; not like himself."

Myrtle said slowly, "All because of Royce's death? That seems a little odd to me, Cindy. I'd never gotten the impression that Preston cared all that much for Royce. In fact, I remember a lot of high school history—you'd probably be surprised to hear that."

Cindy gave a short laugh. "Miss Myrtle, you were always sharp as a tack. I don't think anything slips by you."

"As I recall," continued Myrtle, "you were dating Royce for a while during your high school years. Then Preston won you over. I believe that probably generated some bad blood between the two men."

Cindy was quiet for a moment and then took a few large gulps of the sherry, draining the glass. Myrtle gave Miles a pointed look, meaning he needed to fill it again and he shook his head. The sherry bottle was empty.

Then Cindy said, "It's true. They didn't like each other." She gave a hiccupping sob and Myrtle looked at her with concern, wondering if she was going to have to find her tissue box. "Oh, Miss Myrtle. I was back with Royce."

"The two of you were having an affair?" asked Myrtle, although she knew good and well that they were.

Cindy nodded miserably. "That's right. It had been going on for a while. Preston . . . oh, I feel just awful about it. But he found out. I asked him to forgive me. He just looked so disappointed and sad. It makes me feel even worse about all of this . . . that he thought poorly of me right before he died."

"You and Preston always seemed happy together when I saw you around town," said Myrtle. "I guess we never really know what goes on in people's private lives, though."

Cindy said, "We *were* happy. That was the thing. It wasn't all a lie. I don't really even know why I ended up seeing Royce again. It wasn't like anything was missing from my relationship with Preston. I guess I was sort of flattered by the attention and it turned my head. Maybe it even made me feel young again, like I was back in high school and having two guys argue over me." She grimaced and held her head with both hands. "I can't believe how stupid I was. Now I've lost everything." She looked up suddenly. "You were there, weren't you? When Preston was . .

. found? Did you get any other information? Did Red tell you anything?"

Myrtle shook her head sadly. "Unfortunately, Red doesn't provide much information. But I guess you already discovered that, since you're asking me."

Cindy sighed. "He just gave me the basics—that Preston's death was suspicious, he was found in Erma's backyard, and they were going to be investigating. Then he asked me a bunch of questions that I didn't have the answer to because I was asleep and because Preston wasn't telling me what was going through his head."

Myrtle said, "Can I do anything for you, Cindy? Bring you some food later today?"

Miles shifted uncomfortably in his chair.

Cindy quickly said, "Oh no, no Miss Myrtle. I'll be just fine, although I appreciate it. You've done more than enough for me just letting me invade your home like this. You have some sort of event going on, too." She cast a doubtful glance toward the front door.

"Oh, just that little fundraiser. All right, but you must let me know if there's *anything* I can do for you."

Cindy stood up, swaying just a bit on her feet, whether from exhaustion or the effects of the sherry. "Thank you. I'm going to get out of your hair now."

And, in a moment, she was gone.

"What do you make of all that?" asked Myrtle, sitting back in her chair.

Miles said, "I think she drank quite a bit of your sherry."

"Well, yes, but she was walking and not driving, and she'd had a terrible shock."

Wanda croaked, "More upset about her guilt."

Myrtle looked at her through squinty eyes. "I presume you're referring to the guilt she feels about Preston discovering her affair with Royce. You're not saying that Cindy is guilty of murdering Preston, are you?"

Wanda shrugged and looked unhappy. "The sight—"

"Yes, yes, the sight doesn't work that way. Which is most unhelpful of it. But I'll agree that Cindy did seem extremely rattled by the fact that Preston had learned of her affair and then died shortly after."

Miles shifted uncomfortably. "You don't think she was *too* despondent, do you? She did make that statement about losing everything. Do you think she's all right being alone right now?"

Myrtle frowned. "Are you asking if I think she's going to do herself harm? I don't think so." She paused, thinking it through more. "But *I'd* be the one feeling guilty if she did. I know what I'll do. I'll call Red."

Miles glanced at the clock and Myrtle said, "Don't be silly, Miles. Red isn't asleep. He's got a new victim on his hands."

She picked up her phone and dialed his number. Red answered and it sounded as if he was right in the middle of a groan. "Mama? Now what?"

"Well, that's not a very nice way to greet your mother, for one. You need to work on your manners."

"I hope you aren't calling me to talk about phone etiquette," growled Red.

"No. I'm calling to let you know that maybe you should send someone along to be with Cindy Cook. She was wandering down our street and came in to visit and she looked decidedly unwell and made a rather hopeless statement while she was here. Perhaps a welfare checkup of some sort?"

Red said, "Cindy Cook just happened to pay you a call right after her husband died."

"I *don't* appreciate that disbelieving tone, Red Clover! It's precisely what happened. She didn't want to be alone and she didn't want to be at home. She drank the rest of my sherry, which Erma had already put quite a dent in, and headed back out into the darkness."

Red sighed. "Okay. I'll let the state police know and see if they can spare an officer to sit with her for a while or make contact with some of her family."

"You're welcome," said Myrtle huffily, hanging up the phone. She narrowed her eyes. "Now I'm especially looking forward to our gnome event this morning."

Miles, however, was not particularly looking forward to the gnome event. He couldn't really imagine that it was going to get much traffic and he had the feeling it would end up being him and Wanda sitting outside munching on potato chips while Myrtle paced around impatiently.

So he was pleasantly surprised when there were cars pulling up and over to the curb and then a line forming at the table. Then he was panicked. He was the photographer and the process meant not only taking the picture, but sending it along to the recipient since he didn't want to use their own, germy phones to take the photos. He quickly discovered that the sending part took a good deal of time since he had to type in the number to text it to or the email address to mail it to.

Myrtle beamed at everyone as they came by. "Welcome! So good to see you. Yes, any sort of donation . . . it goes right in this jar. Now pick a gnome and Miles will take a picture of you."

Honking was also happening as cars went by since Myrtle had put a "honk if you love gnomes" sign out.

Wanda was at first tasked with making sure everyone made a donation and knew where the snacks were. But then Myrtle decided that Wanda was becoming too much of a distraction as once again people were asking her to tell them their fortunes. Myrtle quickly hustled her inside. "Sorry, Wanda," she murmured.

"Not a problem," said Wanda, looking pleased. "I'll play cards."

"And make yourself a sandwich!"

Miles did take quite a few pictures that weren't any good, but since the issues with the photos were quickly discovered, he was able to retake them.

There were a *lot* of children there. Myrtle had expected that. What she hadn't expected was the number of adults there.

One of them said to her in a gleeful tone, "I've always wanted to wander through the gnomes, but I couldn't do it before because it was trespassing."

"Yes, well, all rules are suspended today! Enjoy yourself," said Myrtle.

Elaine came across the street about halfway through the event, with Jack in tow. Jack immediately headed for Myrtle and gave her a big hug around her leg. Both Elaine and Jack were wearing "Vote for Myrtle" stickers.

"Who's the smartest little boy in the world?" asked Myrtle, beaming at him.

"Me!" said Jack. Then he got quickly distracted by the table of goodies behind Myrtle.

"Is it okay if he has a snack?" Myrtle asked Elaine.

"Go for it," she said with a laugh. "He's already had a nutritious breakfast, so might as well eat a little junk. Sorry we couldn't make it here any earlier. I had one thing after another come up."

Myrtle suddenly noticed that both Elaine and Jack were wearing rather odd outfits. Their clothes were both covered with stripes. But the stripes didn't really line up with each other and the entire effect was making Myrtle feel very dizzy. She leaned heavily on her cane as her gaze wandered over them.

Elaine noticed and she said proudly, "What do you think? I've started sewing and I thought it would be so cute for Jack and me to have matching outfits. I picked out the fabric, myself."

Myrtle had no doubt of that. Unfortunately, not only was Jack's shirt a striped mess, it was also apparently itchy. He absently scratched at his shoulder as he watched people posing with the gnomes.

Miles walked up and blinked at the sight of Elaine and Jack. "Hi, Elaine."

Elaine said, "Hi, Miles!" She leaned in and said to them both conspiratorially in a low voice, "I hope you were both able to get some sleep last night after the incident."

Myrtle shook her head. "Unfortunately, there wasn't a whole lot of sleeping going on last night. However, it was rather action-packed. Did Red happen to disclose anything to you?"

Myrtle didn't have a lot of hope that Red had. He'd gotten just as cagey when speaking to Elaine about cases as when he was speaking with Myrtle. That's because Elaine had fallen into what Red considered a bad habit in terms of sharing information with Myrtle.

Elaine shook her head ruefully. "I wish I had more intel. Of course, he bolted out of the bed when Erma was screaming and texted me later to tell me what was going on. He just told me Preston was dead in Erma's yard. Which does seem a little strange. He didn't offer me any ideas about that, either."

Myrtle made a face. "Red has been decidedly unhelpful lately. Very unforthcoming. Well, that's fine. We can get information without his help. Did Erma wake Jack?"

Elaine said, "Believe it or not, no. He slept like a baby last night."

They turned to look at Jack who was happily climbing on a gnome that, inexplicably, had a small dinosaur on a leash.

Miles said hesitantly, "Would you like a picture of you and Jack with the gnomes?"

"I would *love* one," said Elaine. "Where's the jar for the fundraiser?"

Myrtle pointed it out and Elaine joined Jack with the gnome.

"You'll have to have this photo blown up and framed," said Myrtle. "Do promise me, Elaine."

"I absolutely will," she said.

Myrtle smiled to herself. The picture would likely drive Red insane inside his own home, which was precisely the effect she hoped to have. The combination of the dizzying stripes and the gnomes was perfect.

Miles sent the picture to Elaine's phone and then they stood and chatted for a few minutes.

"Where's Wanda?" asked Elaine curiously.

"Oh, we had to shoo her away inside. You know how people are—they start harassing Wanda, trying to hear their fortunes. It's completely draining for the poor woman. But hopefully I can do something fun with her later to get her out of the house. Otherwise, she'll play cards all day long. Puddin got Wanda hooked on game shows, so that's a thing, too."

At that moment, Red's police cruiser went slowly by and Red gaped out the window at the sight of Myrtle's gnome-filled yard populated by people having their pictures taken. Red did *not* honk his horn to show his love of gnomes.

Myrtle watched smugly. "I guess Red didn't hear about my event today."

"Well, he didn't have a chance to read the paper because of Preston's death," said Elaine. "I did see Sloan had included a blurb about your fundraiser. It appears to be quite a success."

Myrtle glanced around and stood a little straighter. "It certainly is."

Elaine said, "By the way, if you send me your measurements, I could make *you* an outfit, too. I know you're always complaining about how your funeral outfit seems to always get spilled on. I could sew together a pantsuit or something for you."

Miles came up just in time to hear this and made a funny coughing sound which he hastily turned into a real cough as Elaine turned his way.

Myrtle drew in a deep breath and said, "That's so lovely of you, Elaine. I'm afraid it might be a little while before I can get those to you, unfortunately. Just with everything going on—the campaign, Wanda, the crime stories I'm writing. You understand, don't you?"

"Sure! Whenever things slow down a little bit, just send your measurements over and I'll take care of the rest."

Myrtle could only imagine what "taking care of it" might entail. She shivered at the thought of the garment that might ensue.

"Well, I'd better run. Jack and I have a lot of errands to do today. Tell Wanda I said hi."

Myrtle called after her, "Remember to print that picture! Make it nice and large!"

Elaine lifted her arm in a wave and walked across the street and into her house.

# Chapter Seventeen

After another forty-five minutes, the event wrapped up. Myrtle took the jar of cash inside and dumped it out on the kitchen table as Wanda left to watch a game show and Miles trailed behind them.

Myrtle counted it all out loud and finally said, "Two-hundred dollars! Wow!" She frowned. "Maybe I really should continue running for the seat. People do seem very enthusiastic about supporting me."

"Or perhaps overly-enthusiastic about having their photo taken with gnomes," said Miles dryly. "By the way, I'm completely exhausted. That was a lot of pressure to put on me."

"Pressure? You were merely taking snapshots, Miles. Everyone loved their pictures."

Miles peered down at the photo gallery on his phone. "Is there a quicker way to delete all these photos instead of doing it one by one?"

"I have no idea. We could give your phone to Jack the next time we see them. He seems to be a genius with technology."

Miles seemed reluctant to offer his phone to a three-year-old.

Wanda said, "Ain't Tippy gonna run?"

"I need to follow up with her. I could do that now . . . and tell her that her country needs her. She does respond well when it's put in terms of duty," said Myrtle. "I could call her now."

Wanda drawled, "She's at the garden center."

"Is she? Goodness but it's helpful having a psychic around. I do believe it might actually be better to ask Tippy in person. It would pressure her just a bit more. Let's all go to the garden center." Myrtle grabbed her purse off the kitchen counter.

Miles groaned. "I just mentioned how exhausted I am."

"You'll rally, Miles. Besides, there's no way that Wanda and I can walk all the way to the plant nursery. We did enough walking yesterday—I think I may have worn my shoes down to a nub."

Miles glanced down at Myrtle's sensible orthopedic shoes. "That's rather unlikely."

"But I could always drive your car if you preferred," said Myrtle sweetly. "My license has been renewed for another ten years."

Miles stood up and took his keys out of his pocket. "I'll drive."

Myrtle said, "Good. Although you know I'm an excellent driver, Miles. I'm not sure I appreciate your concern about my driving your vehicle."

"My concern has something to do with you driving fifteen miles an hour," said Miles.

Myrtle gave him a reproving look. "Nothing bad happens when you drive fifteen miles an hour. It's the safest way to drive. However, I'm happy for you to be the driver today. Wanda, I have a little extra money set aside from my retirement check this month . . . how about if you and I find something small we can buy at the garden center?"

Wanda grinned and nodded happily. Then she looked concerned. "Can we find somethin' cheap there?"

"We certainly can. We'll just avoid shopping in whatever sections Tippy is shopping in. Miles, is there anything you might need there?"

Miles considered this. "I suppose it wouldn't hurt to get some fertilizer."

"An exciting purchase, for sure," murmured Myrtle.

A ten-minute drive later, they arrived at the plant nursery. They could see Tippy outside, looking at some flowering bushes thoughtfully.

Miles said, "There are *two* luxury vehicles here. Who might the other one belong to?"

Myrtle craned her head and gasped. "I think that's Jenny Rollins's car. Isn't it? Oh good . . . maybe we'll have the chance to knock out two birds with one stone."

Wanda said, "Which one first? Cause one of 'em might leave."

"We should *certainly* speak with Jenny first. Tippy appears to be deep in thought and I don't consider her a speedy shopper. Besides, I can always just pop by Tippy's house. It would be a bit more awkward popping over to Jenny's."

Miles said carefully, "I noticed there wasn't any casserole delivery to Jenny's house." He and Wanda exchanged a glance.

Myrtle sighed. "No. No, there wasn't. Jenny said that she already had plenty of food at the house and didn't need any more.

I suppose she doesn't need as much food now that Scotty is out of the house and living on his own. I'm kind of curious to hear how that's going, too."

They walked into the garden center and glanced around for Jenny.

"There she is," whispered Myrtle in her stage whisper. She took off quickly in the direction of the hanging plants as Wanda and Miles followed.

"Good morning, Jenny," chirped Myrtle as she approached the woman.

Jenny looked surprised. "Well, goodness. I seem to keep running into you, Myrtle. It's good to see you."

The last was said in a somewhat-doubtful tone. A tone Myrtle ignored.

"You know Miles, I think. And this is my friend Wanda," said Myrtle.

To her credit, Jenny didn't waver at all at the somewhat-quirky-looking Wanda but extended her hand immediately. "Pleased to meet you."

Jenny seemed composed, as always, but somewhat drained. Her eyes were tired.

Wanda gave Jenny a stern look. "You need to sleep. Don't be up at night no more."

Jenny blinked, looking startled and Myrtle said quickly, "Wanda here is a psychic. Although it doesn't really take a psychic to see that you're sleep-deprived. Are you doing all right, Jenny? Under the circumstances, I mean?"

Jenny nodded, still looking curiously at Wanda. "I'm all right. But I keep hearing noises at night that are keeping me up."

"Noises?" asked Miles, frowning.

"Yes. Oh, it's not really anything—just creaking floorboards, sounds outside the house. Night sounds—you know. Crickets and frogs and whatnot. Maybe the sounds have always been there, but I hadn't noticed them because I felt safe with Royce in the house. Now I'm alone."

Myrtle said, "I was actually just wondering how things were going with Scotty. It sounds like he *did* end up moving out, then? How is he enjoying his new place?"

Jenny gave them her first really genuine smile. "He's so happy. It's the one thing in my life that's really going well right now. Scotty was just so *stuck* before. He didn't finish college or have any kind of vision in terms of what he was going to do next. Now that I've helped him get a little independence by assisting him with rent and letting him move out, everything has changed. He's gotten a job over at the barbeque restaurant."

"He's waiting tables?" asked Myrtle.

"Cashing people out. He enjoys it . . . meeting people and seeing people he knows. I saw him yesterday and he had the biggest smile on his face. It amazed me. I don't know when I'd last seen him smile like that." Jenny said ruefully, "Now, if I can only get my own life straight, maybe he and I will be okay. I guess I need to start with my sleeping." She looked at Wanda and gave her a wry smile.

Myrtle said, "Oh, we're a group that understands sleeplessness here. Well, Miles and I do, at least. I think Wanda's actually a pretty good sleeper. Speaking as someone with many years of insomnia, I'll share my own philosophy toward it, if you like."

Jenny nodded. "Please. I'm starting to think I'm going to have to take something, otherwise."

"Pills are definitely not a good long-term solution. What I do is to try to get up out of bed and do something comforting."

"Comforting?" Jenny looked confused. "You mean like eating comfort food or something?"

"That's one of the things you can do. Sometimes I walk over to Miles's house and have a meal with him."

Miles winced at the thought of the many times he'd actually been sleeping when Myrtle had come over for a nocturnal visit.

"Sometimes I'll work on a puzzle or go for a stroll. It's amazing what one can see when you're out for a stroll."

Jenny wrinkled her brow. "Goodness. You were out last night, weren't you? That couldn't have been very safe, considering what happened at Erma's." In a drained voice she said, "It's so awful that Bradley has these terrible crimes. I'm so worried now about my safety. Do you think it was just some random thing. . . what happened to Preston?"

"No, I can't imagine that. We don't seem to have a lot of just random acts of violence here. I think Preston's death must have been targeted. Of course, what he was doing in Erma's yard is anyone's guess." Myrtle looked at Jenny and said, "You don't have any more ideas about what happened to Royce?"

Jenny sighed. "I don't know. I did remember one thing that happened recently. Bonner and Royce were squabbling."

"More of the construction company dispute?" asked Myrtle.

Jenny shook her head. "I think it was more than that, although at the time I unfortunately couldn't be bothered to listen in. As I told you before, I didn't think Bonner really harbored bad feelings or any real enmity toward Royce. It was simply a business-related argument. But now I'm realizing those two really didn't care for each other. I wish I'd listened more carefully when Royce would talk about their issues. The truth is that sometimes I just pretended to listen . . . nodded at all the right times while we ate dinner. I feel so terrible about that now. But you know how it is." She looked earnestly at Myrtle, Miles and Wanda for affirmation on this point. And the widow, the widower, and the single woman all nodded back at her, although they'd all forgotten or never known.

Jenny looked at Myrtle and said, "Red has been wonderful, Myrtle. I know you must be proud of him."

"Has he?" asked Myrtle sounding a little doubtful.

"He has. I know the spouse is always the main suspect, but Red has really been putting time into thinking outside the box and seeing who might be behind all this. How are he and Elaine doing?"

Myrtle made a face. "Oh, I suppose they're doing fine. Elaine has a new hobby. You know how she likes to keep busy."

Jenny gave another smile. "What is it this time? I know her hobbies are varied and . . . well, I guess they have differing results."

"Sewing." Myrtle sighed. "I'm not sure sewing is Elaine's best hobby. I rather liked her healthy eating one. It was just Red who had a problem with it."

Jenny said thoughtfully, "You know, I'm on a couple of committees at church that I think Elaine would be perfect for. I could give her a call and see if she'd be interested."

Myrtle beamed at her. "That would be wonderful. I appreciate your help, Jenny."

"I'll call her as soon as I'm home. I'm supposed to be getting extra recruits for them anyway. It's been a good way for me to stay busy and distracted."

"Perfect! Because she's already asking me for my measurements and I'm a little concerned to see what kind of outfit she might come up with for me."

Jenny said, "Consider it done."

Myrtle saw Wanda looking over at the hanging plants and quickly said, "We'll see you soon, Jenny. We have a couple of things we wanted to pick up here. Good to visit with you."

Jenny made her way to the checkout counter with her large cart as Myrtle and Wanda carefully read the different instructions on each plant and found a couple that seemed fairly low maintenance.

"You enjoy growing herbs, too, don't you?" asked Myrtle.

Wanda nodded.

"Well, let's start a little herb garden at my house while you're visiting."

Miles frowned. "What are your intentions with an herb garden?"

"My *intentions*? Miles you sound so solemn. I believe our intention is to *eat* the herbs, isn't that right, Wanda? For heaven's sake, we're talking about herbs."

"So you'll be cooking with them?" Miles continued.

Wanda's mouth stretched out into her crooked grin.

"Certainly! If we're able to grow anything at all. Although I believe Wanda has shown herself rather proficient at gardening," said Myrtle.

Miles cast a worried look at Wanda and Wanda croaked, "Herbs is good with scrambled eggs."

Miles suddenly looked a lot more cheerful. "They are indeed! Myrtle's scrambled eggs are the best."

Myrtle looked pleased again. "Why, thank you, Miles! I'll have to remember that for the future. Perhaps you can come over and have breakfast for supper one night. And now we should head over to the herb section, which, if I'm correct is right next to where Tippy is currently shopping."

Tippy was indeed still standing there, looking very thoughtfully at a cherry tree as if trying to envision it in her massive yard.

"Tippy!" said Myrtle cheerfully and Tippy jumped.

"Goodness but you were deep in your thoughts," said Myrtle.

Tippy chuckled and patted her chest as if to possibly jumpstart her heart again. "Yes, sorry, Myrtle. I was just trying to decide whether I wanted to make a purchase or not. How are the three of you doing? Finding some wonderful plants?"

They talked about the hanging plants and the herbs they were going to buy. Then Myrtle purred, "I'm so delighted we happened into each other today, Tippy. I wanted to check back in with you on your candidacy."

Tippy deflated slightly, looking away from Myrtle. "Oh, I don't know, Myrtle."

"Did you speak with Benton about it?" asked Myrtle brightly. In her head, she was concocting all sorts of terrible things to say to Tippy's husband if he'd pooh-poohed the idea.

"Yes, and he was totally onboard with it," said Tippy reluctantly. "I was just wondering if I had the energy to take on town hall."

"Well, you're not really *taking it on*, Tippy. You'll be there to be the grown-up in the room when there are discussions. As you know, the town council is desperately in need of a grown-up. Please, Tippy. It's either you or it's me. And I'm a senior citizen." Myrtle crouched over her cane in an effort to look as decrepit as possible.

Tippy sighed and shook her head with a short laugh. "I can tell you're not in the mood to take no for an answer, Myrtle. If you really feel I'll make a difference, I'll go ahead over to town hall and sign up and get the paperwork."

Myrtle's eyes sparkled. "Wonderful! That's exactly what I was hoping to hear. Believe me, you'll definitely be making a difference. I'll head over to town council with you and take myself *off* the ballot. You'll be pleased to know that my fundraiser this morning brought in quite a bit of money, which I'll be happy to forward over to your campaign."

Tippy didn't appear to be very enthusiastic about this. "I'm not sure that's the correct protocol. Those people were giving money because they were supporting *you* as a candidate, not me."

Miles cleared his throat. "I believe they were giving money because they wanted their picture taken with a gnome."

Myrtle said, "Miles is completely correct. Those folks weren't there for politically-motivated reasons."

"Just the same, I think I'll fund my campaign myself. Just to ensure everything appears on the up-and-up."

"In that case, I'll donate the money to the animal shelter," said Myrtle.

Tippy relaxed a bit. "That sounds like an excellent idea."

"Are you ready to go to the town hall now?" asked Myrtle. She was ready to remove herself from the ballot and get Tippy on it.

Tippy looked longingly around the garden center as if wishing she could spend a good deal more time there. "Well . . . yes. I suppose I could. I can swing back by here afterward."

Wanda was still gazing in the direction of the herbs and Myrtle realized she was being a bit unfair. Wanda was wanting to be like Tippy and just thoughtfully browse around without having to encounter suspects and people who needed to be persuaded to run for office.

"Tell you what, Tippy. How about if you give me a lift to town hall and Miles and Wanda can linger here at the garden center," said Myrtle.

Miles looked less-than-delighted at this plan.

Tippy said, "I can actually drive you back home too, Myrtle. Then Wanda and Miles can take all the time they need here."

Now Miles looked truly despondent. Wanda's eyes had lit up, though.

"Perfect!" Myrtle turned to Wanda, "Now these are both of our purchases, so let me give you some money for it all."

"I have it covered," said Miles, a little stiffly.

Myrtle was never one to argue if someone were offering to pay for anything. "Even better! Thank you, Miles."

# Chapter Eighteen

Myrtle and Tippy headed out to Tippy's roomy Cadillac. Tippy turned on the car and jazz music started playing on the speakers. Tippy, always the perfect hostess, even if she was hosting in her car, started asking Myrtle questions about how Jack was doing and what Elaine was up to. Before Myrtle knew it, they were at town hall.

The town clerk did not look excited to see Myrtle there again.

"I'd like to drop out of the race, BeeBee," said Myrtle. "And Tippy would like to sign up."

BeeBee muttered something under her breath and pulled out a stack of paperwork for Tippy and a separate piece of paper for Myrtle. "Forms and signatures," she said.

Myrtle poised her pen above the paper. "So it's not a problem, then? That Tippy becomes a candidate even though it's post-deadline?"

BeeBee rubbed at her forehead as though it hurt. "No. That's because we currently have no candidates for the seat."

Myrtle frowned. "But there's Erma Sherman."

"Dropped out earlier this morning," drawled BeeBee. "Said there was a troubling incident in her yard and thought it might be politically-motivated."

Tippy gave Myrtle an alarmed look and Myrtle said, "Oh, that's just Erma being hyperbolic. You know how she is."

Tippy said sharply, "Preston's demise didn't have anything to do with Erma running for office, did it?"

"Certainly not! It had to do with Erma having a big mouth at Royce's funeral."

BeeBee was now looking interested. Myrtle said, "I'll fill you in later, Tippy. Just rest assured that you don't have to worry about running for office."

Myrtle waited until Tippy started filling out the forms in her sweeping handwriting and then scrawled her name on the form to withdraw from candidacy.

A minute later, Myrtle decided that the process of signing Tippy up was going to take forever. She was a very careful person and very deliberate in terms of what she put her name to. She was studying the form and asking BeeBee lots of questions and there wasn't anywhere for Myrtle to sit down in the town clerk's office.

"I'll meet you out in the lobby," said Myrtle and Tippy absently nodded.

Myrtle walked out into the lobby and right to a bench. She was getting a peppermint out of her purse when the door to the building opened and Bonner Lang walked in. He started passing Myrtle, seemingly completely focused on heading to the stairs.

"Bonner?" asked Myrtle, calling out in her authoritative voice.

Bonner jumped a little and then gave Myrtle a half-smile. "Why, Miss Myrtle! What an unexpected pleasure to see you here this morning. How are you doing?"

"I'm doing well, Bonner. I have news for you."

"Is it about your campaign? I have to admit I did a little informal polling and there's quite a bit of local support for you as a candidate. I think you might be a shoo-in." Bonner grinned at her.

Myrtle didn't look surprised. "Well, that's not too surprising. After all, I taught many of them. It's not as if no one knows who I am. However, after careful consideration, I have decided to drop out of the race."

Bonner's eyes bugged out. He clearly came from the tradition of never dropping out of anything, especially if he had any kind of support. "Dropping out? Why on earth for? You're not having any health issues, I hope."

Myrtle shook her head impatiently. "Nothing like that. It's just that I had a good conversation with Tippy Chambers and she's decided to run for the council seat. I'm throwing all my support behind her. Besides, she's currently the only candidate."

Bonner's eyebrows flew up.

"The only candidate, Miss Myrtle? Why, I thought Erma Sherman was in the race."

Myrtle shook her head sadly, as if very upset about Erma. "I'm afraid not. You might have heard about the incident last night. Were you out and about last night?"

"I most certainly was *not* out and about last night. I do have one excellent habit that you helped instill in me in my formative years, Miss Myrtle."

Myrtle tilted her head. "What's that?"

"A love of reading. The only thing is that reading at night makes me very, very drowsy. Sometimes I'll drop off in the middle of reading a book and have to re-read a page or two."

"So you wouldn't have heard then," said Myrtle.

"Heard what?"

"That Preston Cook was murdered last night . . . in Erma's yard, actually."

Bonner's eyes bugged out. "You're kidding me."

Myrtle sniffed. "I don't joke around about violent death."

"Why . . . what on earth is going on? As far as I'm aware, Erma and Preston didn't even know each other." He frowned and looked as if he were trying and failing to connect the dots.

Myrtle stepped in to try and help. "Well, Erma seemed to think it had something to do with her running for the council and that's apparently why she's dropped out. But I believe it might have more to do with the remarks Erma was making at Royce's funeral. You were there, weren't you?"

Bonner wrinkled his brow as if trying in earnest to fish this elusive information from his brain. "I was at the funeral. But for some reason, I can't really seem to recall any remarks from Erma. Although she might have mentioned that she'd been suffering some stomach upset."

"She also mentioned that she had important information from the night Royce was killed," said Myrtle.

"Why would she say something like that?" asked Bonner slowly.

"It's typical Erma behavior. She does like the limelight, even if it means outshining the deceased at a funeral," said Myrtle with a sigh. "Still, it doesn't mean she deserved to die because of it."

"*Erma* died, too?"

"No, no. But I'm wondering if the reason Preston was in her yard in the middle of the night was because he was trying to get rid of Erma before she disclosed whatever it was that she knew. How well did you know Preston?" asked Myrtle.

Bonner shook his head. "Not very well at all. No, ma'am. He worked on my car from time to time and we engaged in polite small-talk, but that's about it. I'd hate to think that the man was a killer, though. He sure didn't seem to fit the profile. Now it sounds as if I'm going to have to find a new place to repair my car when it goes on the blink."

He cast a concerned eye out the front of the town hall building to the BMW sedan.

"And nothing has occurred to you as to what might have happened with Royce?"

Bonner said, "Absolutely not. Any talk of some sort of enmity or professional rivalry between us was completely overblown. You can ask Jenny—I've been over there a few times since Royce died to try and help her out. Royce and I were golfing buddies. We'd known each other since forever. Sure, Royce was trying to get under my skin a little for running, but that doesn't mean I'd want to kill him." He paused. "I do have to say that it's odd that Preston was discovered in Erma's yard. You know, Erma took the brunt of Royce's heckling at the debate."

Myrtle quirked a brow. "You think *Erma* might have killed Royce and then Preston?"

"Well, she could have, couldn't she? I'm not saying there was anything deliberate about Royce's death, mind you. But she could have really had her feelings hurt during the debate because Royce was being rather ruthless. Maybe Preston found out about it and went over to Erma's to try and blackmail her or something. Then, instead of paying him, she killed him."

Myrtle considered this. As appealing as the prospect was for Erma to be hauled off to prison, the reality was that Erma was really quite innocuous. She simply didn't have it in her to commit two heinous murders.

She shook her head. "I followed you on that, Bonner, but I just don't see it. No, I think something else is going on. Any other observations?"

"Hm. I suppose I did see Scotty Rollins speaking with Preston at the funeral. Maybe he killed his father in a fit of pique at not being helped financially and Preston knew he'd done it. Then Scotty had to kill him."

Myrtle nodded slowly. "I see. Okay, well, that's an interesting theory. I'll keep that in mind."

Bonner looked as happy as he did when she'd given him a good grade on an essay back in high school.

Tippy finally came out of the town clerk office and smiled as she saw Bonner there. Bonner strode up to her holding out his hand.

"Tippy, Myrtle gave me the news and I'm just as pleased as punch! Welcome aboard."

Tippy shook his hand in her businesslike grip and then said wryly, "Myrtle's put the cart a bit before the horse, although it's true that I have my packet. But I'm a long way from being elected."

Bonner whipped a pen out of his pocket and said, "May I, Tippy?"

Tippy handed him her packet and he signed off on her candidacy. "Miss Myrtle?" he asked, proffering the packet to her.

Myrtle scribbled out her name. "Tippy, you're practically halfway done. Head over to Bo's Diner and you can finish it off and turn it back in."

"I was going to take you back home so Miles didn't have to worry about it," said Tippy staunchly.

"Don't be silly—I can walk home myself. You get your paperwork completed and we'll all feel a lot better."

Myrtle said goodbye and watched as Tippy headed out the door. Myrtle paused because she saw someone on the way in . . . someone she wanted to speak to. It was Polly Switzer, wearing a smile when she spotted Myrtle.

Polly was on the town council and could be counted on to give an accurate picture of what might be going on there.

"Myrtle!" said Polly. "How are you doing? Have you tied up that election yet? I'm looking forward to having another grownup on the council."

"Yes, I'd noticed you were really the *only* adult in the room during those meetings. Sad to say, Polly, but I've decided to drop out. However, the only reason I did is because Tippy Chambers is stepping in. You know she'll do a great job."

Polly, who had looked concerned when Myrtle said she was dropping out, looked instantly relieved at the mention of Tippy. "Yes. Yes, she definitely will. Oh, that's good news, Myrtle."

Myrtle said, "I have a couple of questions for you that only an insider would be able to answer."

Polly grinned at her. "It sounds like Myrtle Clover, Ace Reporter, is on the job again."

"Well, I thought I'd try to figure out what's going on since there hasn't seemed to be a lot of progress on the case so far. What I wanted to know about was Bonner and Royce's relationship."

Polly chuckled. "Let me guess. Bonner made it sound as though he and Royce were the best of friends."

"He certainly did. Oh, he said there were some hurt feelings about the fact they didn't choose Royce's construction company for that big project but continued saying that they still got along just fine and even played golf together."

Polly said, "Well, the issues between Royce and Bonner were a lot more contentious than that. The golf games were, too," she added dryly.

"So you think there were hard feelings between them still? More than just feeling a little piqued?"

Polly nodded her head. "Most definitely. In fact, I was delighted when you stepped into the race because I was really worried about how the council meetings were going to go if Royce won the election. I didn't think I wanted to deal with all the sniping on a regular basis."

Myrtle smiled at her. "Thanks so much. You've given me exactly what I was looking for."

Polly continued walking toward the elevator. "Good to see you, Myrtle. Good luck solving this case."

Myrtle ran into Red on his way to the station. Unfortunately, he appeared to have heard Polly's words before she'd disappeared into the elevator.

He groaned when he saw her. "Mama, I'm starting to feel like I can't escape you. And what sort of nonsense was going on in your yard this morning?"

"It was a lovely fundraiser for my now-defunct campaign."

Red's eyes brightened. "What? You mean you dropped out?"

"You needn't look so gleeful, Red. It was a carefully-calculated decision."

Red said, "I can believe that. Everything you do is carefully calculated. But what made you decide to drop out?"

"Because Tippy Chambers is dropping *in*. I was the mastermind behind that." Myrtle paused. "Perhaps I should be her campaign manager. Oh, never mind. Tippy is so organized, she doesn't require one." She gave Red a sweet smile. "Have you found out any information on the brouhaha last night?"

"If you're referring to the murder that took place next door to you, only a few bits and pieces here and there."

Myrtle raised her eyebrows. "Surprising. Because you appear to have been up all night."

"As, I'm sure, were you," said Red smoothly. "Now, Mama, I really have to go. I'm meeting up with Lieutenant Perkins to go over things."

"Go over things you haven't found out yet? That does sound rather premature. Unless you *have* discovered some information on Preston's murder and are simply reluctant to share it with me. Please give Perkins my regards."

"Just stay out of trouble, Mama, please? Don't think I didn't hear Miss Polly telling you good luck on solving the case. That's the last thing you need to be doing—being nosy and getting the murderer riled up. And no gallivanting around in the middle of the night. This last murder was a little too close to home." Red hurried into the police station inside the town hall.

Myrtle took a thoughtful walk back home. At least, it was thoughtful until Pasha started loping along beside her.

Myrtle stopped and beamed at the black cat. "Pasha! You've been so attentive lately. Are you worried about me? At least you show it in a much more appropriate manner than my son does. I'm glad you're keeping an eye on me."

Pasha half-closed her eyes and gave her rattling purr. She resumed her accompaniment of Myrtle on the stroll back to the house.

Wanda opened the door to them and Pasha wound herself around Wanda's legs as Wanda bent down to rub the cat.

"I'm going to grab some tuna for Pasha. She's being such a good girl and brilliant, too, as always. She knows bad things are happening around here and she's looking out for me," said Myrtle as she headed back to the kitchen.

On the way, she passed by Miles, who had apparently been sleeping in the armchair. He woke with a start and rubbed his eyes.

"Coffee for everyone!" declared Myrtle. "Heavens, Miles, you're looking about as groggy as Red."

Miles chuckled. "So you ran into Red at the town hall? I'm sure he was very happy to see you."

"Delighted, as always! He claimed he'd made absolutely no progress on the case, which is rather hard to believe. I think he must be trying to keep everything under his hat, as usual. Which means I'm going to have to strike out on my own for information once again. Anyway, Tippy is now the candidate we're throwing our support behind because she did get her paperwork. I ran into a couple of others at town hall, too."

Miles took a big sip from his coffee, figuring he was going to be asked to be sharper than he currently was.

"First, I spoke with Bonner, who was genial as always, but not particularly helpful. He spun this yarn about he and Royce being golfing buddies. Said that maybe they had their disagreements, but it hadn't created hard feelings on either side. He did mention Scotty speaking with Preston at Royce's funeral, but that was a silly thing to bring up considering Scotty was speaking with *everyone* at his dad's funeral. It would have been rude not to," said Myrtle.

Miles looked confused. "What was Bonner trying to make of that? Was he saying that Scotty found out Preston knew something about Royce's death and then Scotty killed Preston?"

"I don't think he knew *what* he was saying. I think Bonner was just throwing things out there to see what would stick and deflect attention from himself. Anyway, then I ran into Polly. You remember Polly, Miles." Myrtle turned to Wanda. "Polly is on the council and is sharp as a tack. Polly said that Bonner and Royce most certainly did have hard feelings toward each other and that their golf games weren't that friendly, either."

"Are *anyone's* golf games friendly?" asked Miles. "I remember being dragged out to the golf course and feeling a distinct level of enmity under all the friendly-sounding camaraderie."

"The point is that Bonner is lying," said Myrtle, giving Miles a disapproving look. "We don't need to take this as a statement on golfing as a hobby."

"Aren't they *all* lying?" asked Miles.

"Yes," croaked Wanda.

Myrtle looked at her thoughtfully and had a sip of coffee.

"I'm sure Wanda is right. Everyone is trying to present their own version of the truth. And in each version, they're making sure they're the ones who end up looking innocent. At least I know what our plan is now."

"Were you going to share the plan with us?" asked Miles dryly.

"We're going to go to the barbeque restaurant and see Scotty, of course. We haven't spoken to him for a while. Even though he probably does lie, I don't somehow think he's lying quite as much as everyone else."

Miles didn't seem to like this idea. "Barbeque sauce isn't good for my digestion."

"Fortunately, they have other things at the restaurant, Miles. You could order cornbread muffins or corn on the cob."

"Sounds like a lot of corn," muttered Miles.

"For heaven's sake, Miles! They have collard greens there, too."

Miles looked unhappy but nodded.

"Wanda, do you like barbeque?" asked Myrtle.

Wanda said, "I do. But I ain't gonna go."

"Why on earth not?"

"'Cause I done run out of money," said Wanda. "Won't git another check from Sloan fer a week."

"But I'll pay for it. It's just barbeque."

"You done paid enough lately," said Wanda firmly.

Miles cleared his throat. "It would be my pleasure to pay for the meal, Wanda."

Wanda gave him her crooked smile. "You're a good cousin. But you done paid enough lately too. I'm gonna eat a sandwich outta the fridge and play cards."

Myrtle still feel a bit resistant to this plan, but saw the set of Wanda's jaw and realized she wasn't going to get anywhere. "Well, all right. When I come back, we'll all watch *Tomorrow's Promise* together, all right?"

# Chapter Nineteen

Miles and Myrtle walked out to his car. Myrtle sighed. "I feel like Wanda needs to be in town, don't you? It's been good to have her stay with me for a while. She just seems so isolated when she's out there with that crazy brother of hers. Plus, here in town she eats better and can visit with people and is near medical care if she needs it."

Miles was quiet for a few moments and then said, "That's all true. But I wonder if it's how *Wanda* feels about it."

"You think she misses home?" Myrtle, although she prided herself on her imagination, couldn't seem to picture it—missing the dark, cluttered house in the middle of nowhere. "Misses Crazy Dan?"

Miles shrugged. "It's hard for me to imagine it too, but it's all she's known. Plus, you know how people are when they see her in town. It's like a celebrity appearance. They all huddle around her. It's very tiring."

Myrtle made a face. "Well, that's true. If there's one thing I've learned over my many years, it's that people are often thoughtless and annoying. I'll have to find out what Wanda thinks about all this. I'd been wondering if maybe I could help find her a small duplex or something that she could afford in town. Maybe she wouldn't like that, though."

"I think it's something she should be asked about," said Miles.

Myrtle thought about this on the short ride to the barbeque restaurant. The parking lot for the old building was usually packed, but they'd timed their trip there well and there were only a few cars out front. The restaurant had been there for as long as Myrtle could remember, which was a very long time. It was the kind of local hole-in-the-wall place that didn't exactly exude "fine dining," but offered the best barbeque in the county.

They walked in and waited a moment for their eyes to adjust from the bright sunshine outside to the dim interior. When they did, Miles and Myrtle saw Scotty at the front register, grinning at them.

"Look who's here," he said. "How are things going?"

"Oh, pretty good," said Myrtle. "I spoke with your mother recently and she said that you're doing great. She mentioned you were working here now and that your new apartment was really working out."

Scotty nodded. "Sure is. Hey, let's get you both seated and then I'll have a second to talk. It's quiet in here right now."

They followed him to a booth and Scotty handed them both laminated menus. They placed their order (Miles carefully choosing various vegetables) and Scotty gave it to the kitchen before coming back to the table.

"Are you waiting tables, too?" asked Myrtle.

Scotty said with a smile, "Oh, this time of day I do a little bit of everything but usually, I'm just stationed on the cash register."

Myrtle said, "You seem really cheerful, though, working here in any capacity. Do you like the people you work with?"

Scotty's smile widened. "I just like *working*, period! Don't get me wrong—I miss my dad. What happened to him was awful and it wasn't his time to go. Plus, his death has really wrecked my mom. But there were a few things that ended up working out well for me. Dad had his pride and he thought it would be beneath *him* to have a son who worked retail. Ridiculous, right? He was pushing for me to go back to college and get a business major. No matter what I said, he stood totally firm on it."

Myrtle nodded. "Now you're able to be out of the house and making some money of your own. You have your independence and freedom. I completely understand that. My independence is one of the greatest things I treasure."

"I'm so much happier now and feel so much more satisfied with my life. When I was living with my parents and stuck at home, I was frustrated all the time. I mean—I went to several different universities. My grades were totally mediocre and the whole time I was there, I felt lost and kind of directionless. It made it worse that everyone around me seemed to know what they wanted to do and were focused on taking classes and studying to get a step closer every time. I felt like I was the only one on campus who didn't have any kind of plan."

Myrtle said, "Well, I'm so glad that you have a fresh start now, regardless of the circumstances behind it."

Their food arrived and Scotty said, "Let me go grab your plates real quick." He came back with a barbeque plate for Myrtle and Miles's food.

Myrtle took a big bite of her barbeque sandwich and washed it down with her tea. "Let's see, where was I? Oh, I know. It's good to hear you're doing so well, Scotty, but you mentioned your mother isn't? Is there something I can do for her? Does she need food?"

Scotty quickly shook his head. "No, there's actually plenty of food at the house. I think the ladies from the church keep coming by and bringing more. I have a lot in my freezer at my apartment, too. As far as Mom goes, she's doing okay but not great. I mean, she's eating a little bit and seems to be sleeping some. I went by the house last night after work to pick up some stuff that I'd forgot to pack. My shift ended late and I helped to clean up before they closed but I figured Mom would still be awake because she'd had such a tough time sleeping. But I was glad I used my key because she was out like a light. I could even hear her snoring as I went by her room to get the stuff I needed upstairs."

Miles was pushing his vegetables around on his plate instead of eating them which distracted Myrtle. She frowned at him for a moment, before remembering the point of why they were there. "I'm happy to hear that, Scotty. It's been such a crazy time. Did you hear about Preston Cook?"

Scotty said, "Somebody here at work was talking about it earlier. I didn't know who he was. But it's weird that he was murdered. Now when I'm locking up late here, I'm going to be keeping an eye on my back. Hope the police chief figures out who's doing this soon." He tilted his head to one side and looked at Myrtle. "You're his mom, right? Do you know if he's said anything about Foley Hardy? Remember how I was telling you about him? How he was always hanging around Dad?"

Myrtle said, "The only thing I've heard is that he might have owed your dad some money."

Scotty sighed and rolled his eyes. "Dad was gambling again? He'd have torn into me if *I'd* been doing something like that, but for some reason, he thought it was fine for him to do it."

Miles crinkled his forehead. "What kind of gambling was he doing?" Miles apparently had visions of Vegas-style blackjack or roulette wheels rampaging through his head.

Scotty shrugged. "Poker, mostly. At least he was good at it and won most of the time. So you've heard that Foley owed Dad money and that's why he was following him around? Seems like Foley would have been trying to avoid him, instead."

Myrtle said, "Apparently, Foley was trying to convince your father to give him a break on paying him back his gambling debt. Does that sound like something your dad would do?"

Scotty snorted. "No, it doesn't. Like I've mentioned before, Dad wasn't exactly this kindhearted person. Well, you saw that in action yourself, I'm sure. You saw him during the debate."

Miles said slowly, "But you weren't at the debate, were you?"

Scotty reddened a little. "I wasn't there for very long. I didn't want him to think I was trying to be the supportive son, or anything, especially since he hadn't been the supportive dad. But I stuck my head in the door just long enough to hear him giving Erma Sherman a hard time. He didn't look real good doing it." Scotty smiled at Myrtle. "I liked the way that got you fired up."

Myrtle took a sip of her sweet tea. "Somebody has to stand up for Erma for time to time. So you were at the debate."

"Very briefly," Scotty said quickly.

"And then you went back home?"

"I beat the weather back," said Scotty. "Plus, like I said, I didn't want Dad to see me there and think I was the proud son." He paused. "Although maybe, considering the circumstances, I should have done that."

Myrtle shook her head and briskly said, "There's no reason to feel guilty about that, Scotty. You didn't know he was going to die."

Scotty nodded, and seemed to be taking her advice to heart. The bell on the restaurant door rang and he gave them a rueful look. "Good talking to both of you. I guess that's my signal to stop running my mouth." He walked over to seat the customer.

Myrtle took the last couple of bites of her barbeque and said, "Miles, you really didn't eat your vegetables."

Miles was still morosely pushing them around on his plate. "Somehow they still taste of barbeque sauce. I'm getting heartburn just in proximity to them."

"For heaven's sake. I'll get a to-go box and we'll take them home to Wanda."

"Is Wanda a big vegetable eater?" asked Miles.

"Wanda eats everything," said Myrtle. "And quite a bit of it."

They got the to-go box and left as several other diners came in. "Back to your house?" asked Miles.

"Yes. I think I may give Foley Hardy a quick call and have him meet us there."

Miles raised his eyebrows. "You're not hiring Foley directly, are you? Won't that make Dusty upset? He'll think Foley is poaching on his territory."

"Pooh. He'll be glad not to do the work. But I'll have to call Dusty to get Foley's phone number." Myrtle climbed into Miles's car and dialed Dusty's number.

He answered the phone, howling, "Too wet ter mow, Miz Myrtle!"

"I thought you might say something like that, Dusty. That's precisely why I need you to give me Foley's phone number." Myrtle gave Miles a smirk. Maybe Dusty *would* get a little jealous.

Dusty paused. When he spoke again, his voice sounded suspicious. "What you need that fer?"

"My event is over and I thought I may have Foley put a few of the gnomes back up. Not *all* of the gnomes, by any means, but some of them."

Dusty grunted. "Prob'ly a good idea. Them is killin' the grass, especially that giant one."

"Right. So . . . the phone number?"

Dusty gave it to her. Then, apparently trying to sell Myrtle on his own superior qualities as a yardman, he added, "You got ter go git him, you know. Pick him up. Car's broke."

Myrtle sighed. She had indeed forgotten about Foley's car problem. "I'm presuming you know where he lives, since you've been picking him up." She jotted down the address in her little notebook. "That's fine. All right then, Dusty, I'll talk to you later."

She could hear him still muttering as she hung up. She turned to Miles. "We're going to have to make a detour to pick up Foley Hardy."

Miles said, "Ah. The car that doesn't work."

"Exactly." She gave Miles the directions to Foley's house after putting it in her GPS.

"That's more than a detour," groaned Miles. "He lives out in the country."

"It will be a scenic drive," said Myrtle firmly. "We always say we want to get out more."

"Yes, but not out *there*. It's not as if we live in a city and we're yearning for clean air. We're yearning for excitement."

Myrtle said impatiently, "And we'll get it. Foley Hardy might be a two-time killer, for all we know. We get to ride in a vehicle with him."

"Lucky us," muttered Miles.

Foley's house was indeed out in the country. It was, in fact, in the middle of nowhere in the country. There weren't even any nearby farms or old gas stations or anything. He lived in an old house that still appeared to be carefully maintained. A dog of indeterminate heritage watched them suspiciously from the front yard.

Miles said, "I don't like the looks of that dog."

"We'll give him a wide berth," said Myrtle, already opening the car door. "He's probably not used to having many visitors out here."

This was apparently the case because the dog leaped up and bounded toward Myrtle, barking ferociously. Myrtle slammed her car door shut again.

Miles looked wryly at her.

"I suppose we'll just have to let Foley come to us." Myrtle shrugged.

"Do we even know Foley is home? Shouldn't we have just called first?"

Myrtle said, "But where else would he be? He doesn't have a car. There isn't exactly any public transportation out here in the middle of nowhere. I don't think he took a walk for his health. Look, he's coming out the door now."

Foley was. And he wasn't alone—he had his trusty shotgun with him.

"We need to leave, Myrtle." Miles was now speaking in earnest as he started up the car again.

But Foley was putting his hand up to shade his eyes in the bright sun. Then he was smiling and pointing the shotgun down.

"See? He's friendly enough," said Myrtle.

Miles began muttering under his breath again.

"Miles, your muttering has really become a bad habit. Now, roll the windows down so we can have a conversation with Foley."

Foley looked quite cheerful now and eager to talk. It was obvious he didn't get much company out here. But then, between the welcome provided by the dog who was still snapping his teeth at the car and his shotgun, still held tightly in his right hand, it was no wonder.

"What are y'all doing out here?" asked Foley with a big grin. "This ain't on the way to anywhere."

"We came out here specifically to see you," said Myrtle loudly over the barking dog.

"Down, King, down," said Foley, in an attempt to get the big dog off of Miles's sedan. The dog quieted down, looking sulkily at his owner. "King ain't used to visitors."

"I can imagine. I'm sorry we didn't call you first to let you know we were on our way. It was a sort of spur of the moment decision," said Myrtle, quite truthfully. "I wanted to see if you could do a little gnome-moving in my yard."

Foley's eyebrows arched in surprise. "Them gnomes? The ones I pulled out a couple of days ago?"

"That's right. The event I had them out for is over and Dusty has stated that I'm killing my grass. There are days when I feel life might be easier if I *did* kill it all, but I suppose I'd have to hand in my garden club membership if I did."

"Not that that would be a bad thing," pointed out Miles helpfully.

"Just the same, I think I'll keep my lawn alive for right now. I don't want all the gnomes to be put up, just about fifteen percent of them." She frowned and carefully searched Foley's features to make sure that percentages registered in his brain.

They appeared to. He nodded. "Got it." He paused. "But won't it make Dusty mad?"

"It would make Dusty mad if you took over my yardwork. But Dusty doesn't exactly enjoy lugging my gnomes around. He seemed fine with taking a break from it today."

"You're okay to drive me there?" asked Foley.

"Absolutely. We'll give you a ride home, of course," said Myrtle smoothly.

Beside her, Miles groaned quietly.

Foley said, "Thank you. But I'll get my own ride home or crash with my buddy in town. There's some card-playin' goin' on tonight."

Myrtle's expression was severe. "Don't you think you should perhaps consider abstaining from card games? In light of the recent events?"

Foley squinted at her as if trying to follow along. "Oh, you're talkin' about Royce."

"I'm talking about losing money," corrected Myrtle.

Foley bobbed his head. "See, that's what you wouldn't get. It's time for luck to run my way, Miz Myrtle. I've had a spell of bad luck and now it's time for a good spell. If I have a good night, I can take a little money and make it into a lot more money. Pay fer my car repairs."

"Oh, conversely, you could lose the little bit of money."

Miles didn't seem to like the fact that Myrtle was beginning to argue with a gun-toting man. "Myrtle, perhaps we should let Foley have a minute to get ready and then he can get in the car? We could continue the conversation then."

"I'm good to go now," said Foley, reaching out a hand for the door handle.

Myrtle said sternly, "Perhaps you should put your firearm away first. This is a weapon-free vehicle."

Foley looked sheepishly down at his gun. "Kinda forgot it was there."

A minute later, Foley got into the car and they set off.

# Chapter Twenty

Myrtle decided to immediately launch into talking about Preston's death. "Have you heard the news?"

"Not much of a news watcher," admitted Foley. "Also, the TV is broke."

Myrtle said, "You remember Preston Cook."

"Sure. His garage is where my car's at." Foley turned from looking out the window to look at Myrtle in the front seat.

"He's been murdered," said Myrtle.

"What? No way."

"I'm afraid so," said Myrtle.

Foley gave a low whistle. "Ain't that the craziest thing? What am I goin' to do now? I was thinking if I got a used car cheaper than repairin' my old wreck then I'd run it by Preston's place to have him check it out before I bought it."

Miles said, "There are a couple of other places in town, aren't there? Maybe one of them could help."

Foley snorted. "Them? They ain't no good. Preston was the only good one in Bradley. Them others is either bad mechanics or crooked. Maybe I can go out of town to find somebody."

"And you, of course, had nothing to do with Preston's demise, I suppose?" asked Myrtle.

Foley blinked at her and Myrtle added demurely, "It's just that I'm quite particular about who moves my gnomes."

"No ma'am, I had nuthin' to do with it. Like I said, I needed Preston around. Besides, Dusty has me so wore out that I go home and drop into bed. Don't even have the energy to go out and get a drink or nuthin'."

Myrtle asked, "So you weren't out last night then?"

"Nope. Dusty ran me by the store to pick up some soup for supper and then drove me home."

"But you were on your way to see Royce the night he died. Did you speak with him?" Myrtle turned in her seat to get Foley's full reaction.

Foley's full reaction was to turn quite pale and get very still. "What?"

"It's just that there was a witness who places you at the town hall when Royce died. So you clearly didn't go straight home from Preston's garage after you spoke with him about the car."

Miles watched Foley in the rear-view mirror.

Foley spread out his hands in supplication. "Look. I did nuthin' to Royce. But I really needed that money. I did go over there, okay? Knew he was there and the guy was hard to get ahold of. I just asked him to give me more time to get him the money. Or just forgive the debt. Wasn't like the man didn't have no money."

"So when he turned you down, again, you didn't kill him out of frustration?" asked Myrtle, raising her eyebrows.

"No ma'am! I figured I just was flat out of luck again. Called Dusty and went home." He frowned. "Who is it who has it in for me so bad? It's that Scotty, ain't it? He always seemed to show up whenever I was around his dad."

"Did you see him at the town hall?" asked Myrtle, practically turning all the way around.

"Nope. But I saw him yesterday evenin' when Dusty ran me by the store. Saw him leave that barbeque joint."

Myrtle glanced at Miles. Scotty had said that he'd worked late last night so why had Foley seen him out in the early evening?

When they got back to Myrtle's house, Foley set about hauling fifteen percent of the gnomes back to the storage shed while Myrtle and Miles joined Wanda inside. Wanda was playing solitaire.

"How'd it go?" she asked.

Myrtle shrugged. "Well, it seems that no one is inclined to tell us the truth, which isn't very helpful."

Miles said, "Or we're just getting conflicting accounts. You know how eyewitnesses can be. I keep reading in the newspaper how their accounts can be really inaccurate."

"It doesn't help when people are lying. No, Miles, I appreciate your trying to be generous but I think it boils down to the fact that most of the folks we talk to are trying to obfuscate."

Wanda glanced out the window as Foley, looking rather red in the face, went by with a couple of gnomes. "See that Foley is back."

"Yes, and we spoke to him on the way back. He says that Dusty dropped him by the store to pick up soup for supper before taking him back home last night."

Wanda asked, "Could he have come back to town?"

Myrtle shook her head. "Not without some sort of help. His car is in the shop and he lives even more remotely than you do, Wanda. And that's really saying something. He's either lying about having gone home or he got a ride back to town. I hardly think Dusty would have been in the mood to do that much driving back and forth, even if Foley *has* been helpful."

Miles said, "Foley also managed to contradict Scotty's account of where he was last night."

Myrtle sighed. "It's all very vexing. Scotty says he was working late last night and went to his mother's house to collect some things he'd left there. He said she was sound asleep. However, Foley says he saw Scotty leaving the barbeque restaurant in the early evening when Dusty was driving him to buy soup for dinner."

"You could check it," said Wanda in her grating drawl.

Miles said, "Wanda's right. You could call up the barbeque restaurant and confirm that Scotty actually worked late last night."

"All right. I think I'll do that. I can always just hang up if I get Scotty on the line."

Miles said, "They may think you're being really nosy, though."

Myrtle snorted. "They won't think twice about it. That's one of the very best things about being an octogenarian. Everyone just thinks you're a crazy old lady . . . but completely innocuous."

In fact, Myrtle decided to use her best little old lady voice when she called the barbeque restaurant. When a young woman picked up, she said, "Hi . . . I was in just a little while ago eating a late lunch and had such a nice conversation with that lovely young man, Scotty. I was thinking maybe I could do that again."

The young woman, perhaps thinking Myrtle sounded a little lonely, said cheerfully, "Of course you could, darlin.'"

"Could you let me know when his shifts were?" asked Myrtle in her most elderly sounding, tremulous voice.

The young woman consulted a calendar and then rattled off a list of upcoming shifts.

"That's very helpful," said Myrtle sweetly. "Oh, and I thought I saw Scotty out last night, but I wasn't sure it was him. I waved at him, but he didn't wave back. I *do* feel foolish when I wave at the wrong person. Could you tell me what his shift last night was, just to relieve my mind?"

"Sure, sugar. He worked an early shift yesterday. Got off right before the dinner rush started up."

"Thank you very much," said Myrtle. "You've been most helpful."

"Are you his granny?" asked the young woman with some interest.

"Oh no, no. Just a friend of his mother's." Myrtle hung up quickly before any other questions might crop up. "I have the feeling she might be telling Scotty that I called."

Miles shrugged. "You didn't identify yourself."

Myrtle snorted. "I believe he'll be able to figure it out."

There was a knock on the door and Myrtle glanced in that direction in surprise. "Visitors? I was thinking we'd just hang out and watch *Tomorrow's Promise*."

"It's Puddin," said Wanda.

Myrtle, walking toward the door, turned to give Wanda a look of admiration. "Your psychic skills are really helpful, Wanda."

Wanda drawled, "Naw. I just heard Dusty's truck. An' Dusty wouldn't be helpin' with the gnomes."

"Excellent point." Myrtle opened the door and sure enough a sour-looking Puddin stood slouching on the front porch.

"I wasn't really expecting to see you today," said Myrtle. "But I'm not one to look a gift horse in the mouth, either."

Puddin turned and picked up a large tote bag that was full of cleaners.

Myrtle gaped at it. "You mean you actually brought your own cleaners?"

Puddin shrugged a shoulder, her dour, pale face wearing a most annoyed expression. Dusty gave the horn a gentle honk and Puddin waved him off, angrily and stomped inside the house. Dusty, being ensured Puddin was inside, drove away, his engine . . . indeed, the entire truck . . . clanging and thumping.

Puddin slapped the tote bag onto Myrtle's coffee table and gave the assembled group a belligerent look.

Myrtle said, "I'm going to guess that Dusty put you up to this today."

Puddin raised her chin but didn't say anything.

"Sworn to secrecy, are you? I have the feeling that the fact I collected Foley for gnome duty rattled Dusty. He wants to make sure that I realize the value in my current yard and housekeeping crew."

Puddin looked sullen, but didn't dispute this.

Myrtle, however, had ways of making Puddin talk. "I will say that Foley has been most helpful. He's provided all sorts of information that have helped me with these murder cases."

Now Puddin looked even more irritated. She was the one who liked to have information. "Foley's not all-that," she hissed.

"I'll tell you how *you* can be helpful, Puddin. You can actually put a little elbow-grease into your cleaning. When you left last time, there was still a lot of mess to be cleaned up. In fact, I'm not at all sure that you didn't *cause* some of the mess in the process of trying to clean it up. I was seriously thinking that hiring your cousin Bitsy might be worth exploring."

Puddin narrowed her eyes. "Bitsy's too pricey."

"Yes, but people pay her price because she does a good job and she's reliable," said Myrtle. "As long as one can overlook the fact that Bitsy is a terrible gossip."

Puddin said spitefully, "Bitsy's gonna price herself out of a job."

"I suppose some people will pay for quality," said Myrtle. "Not everyone is on a retired teacher's budget."

Puddin's expression was dark but then suddenly brightened and she looked smug. "I know sumthin' Bitsy tole me. About Jenny Rollins."

Miles asked, "Bitsy works for Jenny?"

Puddin beamed at him. "She does. An' she tole me that Jenny is done broke up to pieces."

"All right. Well, there are different ways of being broken-up. Is she referring to physical or psychological or emotional issues?" asked Myrtle.

Puddin looked at her with dislike. "That Jenny is cryin' a lot. All the time. Bitsy's been runnin' the vacuum all the time so she don't have to hear it when she's there."

Myrtle frowned. "That's rather surprising. She seems so very calm and pulled-together when she's in public."

"Hides it well," croaked Wanda.

Puddin suddenly switched her attention over to Wanda. "You been watchin' them game shows we was lookin' at?"

Wanda nodded. "Sometimes."

Puddin said, "I *still* think you need to go on one of them. You'd make money—bein' a witch an' all."

Myrtle grated, "She's *not* a witch, Puddin. She has psychic powers. There's a huge difference. Now, if you've come to clean, maybe you'd better get to it."

Puddin walked toward the closet that held the vacuum and Myrtle said, "But *don't* vacuum first. We want to watch our show."

Miles, as usual, flinched at the mention of the soap opera although he'd expressed interest to Myrtle earlier in seeing one of the weird love triangles on the show resolved.

Myrtle got out the remote, turned on the television, and started up the recording. Wanda curled up on the sofa with Pasha, who had leapt through the kitchen window and sought her out. Miles pushed his glasses up on his nose and looked as if he might be trying really hard to pay attention to the soap opera so that he wouldn't miss anything.

Ten minutes into the show, Myrtle looked behind her to see Puddin leaning in the kitchen doorway, blatantly watching the soap opera. "I'm not paying you to watch TV!" fussed Myrtle.

"Done in the kitchen," said Puddin in a sullen voice.

"Then clean up my fridge. It doesn't have a lot of food in it right now, so it should be a pretty easy job." Then Myrtle turned back around and became absorbed in the show.

After it wrapped up, Myrtle sat looking thoughtfully at the television. "That was really thought-provoking."

"I never considered this particular program very thought-provoking," said Miles. "It's mostly good for entertainment value."

"On the contrary, I think it's quite educational," said Myrtle.

Wanda gave her a perceptive look and nodded her head.

"See? Wanda gets it," said Myrtle.

Miles looked baffled. "Gets what? What sort of insights are you deriving from this soap opera? All I got out of it was that having multiple affairs at once can lead to a lot of complications in your life."

"Love," croaked Wanda.

"Exactly," said Myrtle, beaming at Wanda. "The show is about love."

Miles furrowed his brows. "All right. I don't think it's about love as an ideal, though. It's a bit more tabloid-like than that."

"Yes, but underlying everything is love. Different types of love. And that's what we're looking at with this case, isn't it?"

Miles said slowly, "I suppose so. There's Cindy. I can't quite figure her out. Who did she really love—Preston, the football hero who later became her husband? Or Royce, who she dated in high school and later engaged in an affair with?"

"That's easy. She loves *both* of them. Her heart is big enough. But now, she's full of guilt and she's lost both men," said Myrtle.

"Workin' a lot," said Wanda.

"Well, that's good. I was wondering what she was going to do now. Maybe work can help her make it through this time," said Myrtle. "But that's not the only love story going on with these murders."

Miles offered, "Jenny? We heard she had a very protective approach to Royce and Puddin just said she's been very upset over Royce's death."

"Precisely. She obviously cared a lot about Royce. But I don't think that excludes her from killing him if she was really upset when finding about his affair with Cindy. It could have been one of those things where she found out about it, lashed out, and spontaneously pushed Royce down the stairs. Maybe one of the reasons she's so upset about Royce's death now is because she feels guilty."

Miles said, "What about Preston? He's the one I can't really figure out in this whole mess. I keep thinking that everything would have been explained with Royce's death if Preston wasn't a victim. Then it would have been nice and neat—we'd have known that Preston killed Royce because he was furious that Royce was having an affair with Preston's wife. But with Preston dead, it doesn't make sense."

Myrtle said, "I really hate to say this, but I keep thinking that Erma must know something. I know when I spoke to her on the phone that she sounded clueless but maybe now that a little time has passed, she might realize she knows something important."

Miles groaned and even Wanda made a face. Miles said, "Erma so rarely does."

"I know, but this time it really might be different. Perhaps I should go over there." Myrtle squared her shoulders as if facing an attack.

Wanda croaked, "Maybe you should have a way to git outta there fast."

"An excuse perhaps. Or maybe an excuse to get over there and then get out." Myrtle snapped her fingers. "A casserole! I could bring her a casserole."

Miles frowned. "One of your casseroles-for-the-grieving? But she's not grief-stricken."

"This time it will be a sorry-there-was-a-body-in-your-yard-casserole." Myrtle walked into the kitchen and opened the fridge door and her pantry for inspiration. "Unfortunately, the cupboards are looking rather bare. I'm not sure Puddin did a great job wiping down the fridge, even so."

Puddin, apparently listening in to everything from a distance, hollered from the direction of the bedrooms, "I done a good job!"

Myrtle perused the choices, ignoring Puddin completely. "I suppose I could do a cream-of-something soup and a selection of vegetables. I could call it vegetable pie."

Miles looked rather stricken at this.

"I'll just throw it together real quick. It'll be done in forty-five minutes. You two can find something else to do, can't you?"

Miles obediently tackled the Sudoku in the newspaper. Wanda started playing solitaire. Myrtle preheated the oven and then opened some canned vegetables, drained some of them and forgot to drain others, mixed them in a casserole dish along with a can of cream of celery soup, and stuck it into the oven.

Later, the pungent aroma indicated the casserole was done. Myrtle pulled it out of the oven and Miles and Wanda walked over to take a look at it.

"Maybe I should even call it modified shepherd's pie," said Myrtle.

"What did you throw in there?" asked Miles, looking at the casserole distrustfully.

"Whatever I had in the kitchen. Creamed corn, canned beans of various sorts, some diced tomatoes. Carrots, I think." Myrtle shrugged. The point of the exercise, to Myrtle, hadn't been what was going in, the point was filling up the dish with various vegetables.

"Maybe some cheese on top?" asked Wanda.

"Good idea," said Myrtle. She couldn't find her shredded cheddar so substituted some Swiss cheese slices she found in a drawer in the fridge. She laid them on top of the dish and stuck it back in the oven for a few minutes.

When it was done, Myrtle asked, "Does anyone want to go over to Erma's with me?"

Miles shuddered and shook his head. Wanda reluctantly said, "I'll go if you want me to."

Myrtle sighed. "No, it's fine. I don't know why I thought anyone *would* want to go there. Anyway, if we all go, it may be harder to extricate ourselves. Erma is so very nosy."

Miles and Wanda shared a surreptitious look. Myrtle was rather nosy, herself.

So Myrtle placed the casserole in a tote bag and walked bravely across the lawn to Erma's house. She knocked firmly on the door before she could back out.

# Chapter Twenty-One

There was a small shriek from inside and then a trembling hand pushed the blinds to the side to peer cautiously out the window. Myrtle gave a small wave and managed a smile.

Erma swung the door open wide. "Goodness, Myrtle, you about scared the life out of me."

"By knocking on the door?" Myrtle walked inside.

"Yes! Well, you can imagine I'm on edge after what happened with Preston." Erma sat down on her sofa, pushing a variety of medical-related looking devices out of the way and covering herself up with a large, bright-pink blanket. Then she stared at the bag in Myrtle's hands. "Ooh. Did you bring something for me?"

Myrtle set the tote bag down on Erma's coffee table on top of a stack of very old-looking magazines. "Yes. It's a vegetable pie. Sort of a modified shepherd's pie."

Erma said, "Well, thanks. I'll have to try it later."

Myrtle didn't want to get into one of Erma's extended health-related conversations, but she did feel that all of the medical paraphernalia perhaps needed to be addressed. "Are you feeling all right?" she asked, gesturing at the collective equipment.

Erma's eyes lit up at the opportunity to jump into her favorite subject. "Oh, I'm sort of poorly. It's one reason why I dropped out of the campaign, Myrtle. The doctor said it's the stress—I'm sure you can understand. Can you imagine the horror of finding a body out in your backyard? And then the realization that the body was probably there in the first place to attack you?" Erma shuddered and grabbed a large pill bottle, shaking out a couple of capsules and washing them down with a large glass of water. She glanced back at Myrtle. "I guess you'll be the new town councilwoman."

Myrtle shook her head. "No. No, I dropped out, too."

Erma gave her a wide, delighted, toothy grin. "Really? Did you? Was that to show solidarity?"

"Oh, I guess it was for a variety of reasons. One of them was that once Tippy started running for the open spot, I decided she'd do a fine job."

Erma nodded solemnly. "I didn't realize she'd become a candidate."

Myrtle said, "I did want to check up on you and bring you some food, of course, but I also wanted to see if you'd thought of anything that might be helpful in catching the perpetrator. Have you come up with anything that might give us a lead? Or have you spoken to anyone who could shed a little light on any of this?"

Erma wrinkled her brow. "No, and it's all I can think about. I keep running over and over in my head what happened after the debate. Then I start thinking about Preston in my yard and whether I saw or heard anything that would help. But I can't."

Erma, like Puddin, also liked being someone who knew things. This, of course, was likely the entire reason she ended up with a body in her backyard. If she hadn't been bragging about knowing information, no one would have tried to eliminate her.

Myrtle gritted her teeth in a grin. "You haven't had any glimmers of an idea? You were there at the town hall when Royce was killed. Has anything about that night occurred to you?"

Erma looked as if she very badly wanted to say yes. Then she slowly shook her head. "Nope. Not a thing. But Myrtle, it was pouring cats and dogs and I was really focused on just that one thing—my medic alert bracelet. I didn't *know* there was a killer running around." Then she looked pleased with herself as if something had suddenly come to mind. She added in that smug voice of someone who knows something, "But guess who I *did* talk to? No, you'll never guess! It was Cindy Cook."

As hard as Myrtle tried not to be obviously surprised by anything Erma said since it only encouraged her, this did surprise her. "Did you go see Cindy?"

"No, of course not! Go to the house of someone who tried to kill me? Even if he's dead now, there's no way I would do that." Erma gave a shudder that shook her jowls around. "Cindy came to see *me*."

"Why would she do that?" asked Myrtle.

Erma shrugged. "She felt bad that her husband was going to kill me, I guess."

"Is that what she said?"

"No, no. But it had to be the reason. Anyway, she was trying to get information from me, too, and I just don't have any." Erma's face indicated that this was a tremendous disappointment to her. "She even tried to go over the night Royce died with me, step-by-step, so I could relive it and see if I could remember anything. She seemed practically desperate for information from me." Erma smiled at the pleasant memory.

Myrtle said, "It's not a bad idea. Let's try it."

Erma's face dropped. "But I don't remember."

"Well, I'd also like to hear what Cindy's step-by-step was. Did she go through her evening with you, too?" asked Myrtle.

"A little bit. But not as much as I went through mine. Let's see." Erma looked up thoughtfully upwards as if the conversation might be written up on the popcorn ceiling. "She said she came home from work and started making supper."

"Preston was home with her, apparently." Myrtle recalled Cindy's and Preston's alibi.

"No! No, she was by herself and waiting for Preston to come home from the garage."

Myrtle frowned. "Okay. Well, maybe this is a bit earlier in the evening, then. Preston did work a little late because he was having a conversation with one of his customers." And Foley had been trying to convince him to fix his car without being paid.

"I told her that I was at the debate and that Royce was being rude." Erma flushed a blotchy red at the memory. "That's really all I remember about the debate except that it went on and on and that Royce was rude." She stopped suddenly and beamed at Myrtle. "And you were rude back to him."

Myrtle shook her head. "He was insolent. I was blunt. There's a difference."

"Anyway, so then I told her I was talking to some people after the debate. I was showing people my new medic alert bracelet." Erma fondly fingered the bracelet, which was on her wrist. "Royce was talking with some people, too. I saw that you had left with Miles and Wanda."

"Yes. Wanda was entirely too popular. Plus, we wanted to try to beat the bad weather. Miles isn't fond of driving in storms."

"The storm was awful! I hate driving in weather like that. I had the windshield wipers going full-speed and I still couldn't see anything. Cindy said that when Preston came home, he was totally soaked. I took my huge umbrella. Do you have a huge umbrella, Myrtle? One of those golf umbrellas? They're the best."

Myrtle shook her head. "They're too awkward when you carry a cane. And a little heavy. I have a compact one."

"Okay. Well, anyway, I told Cindy that I saw headlights coming or going. But you know—I was really just focused on trying to find my stuff and get back home. I didn't know anything bad had happened so I wasn't paying a whole lot of attention. I remember the parking lot at town hall was pretty empty and that's most of what I remember." Erma looked a little deflated at this. "Maybe you can help get the word out that I *don't* know anything . . . at least this time. I don't want anybody else sneaking into my yard in the middle of the night to kill me."

Myrtle said briskly, "I'm sure there's not a huge line of people trying to do that, Erma. But I'll be happy to spread the news that you have no idea what happened that night." Myrtle decided grimly that it would be her distinct pleasure to do so. She'd just wasted quite a bit of time making Erma a casserole and coming over for a visit. She stood up. "I'm going to let you go, now, Erma."

Erma said, "Okay. Hey, thanks for the casserole. I sort of thought you weren't a good cook but it smells kind of good. I'm going to have some now, I think."

Myrtle frowned. "I'm not sure where you got the impression that I couldn't cook. I cook quite frequently and no one complains about it."

Erma gave her donkey-like laugh. "I see. Okay, Myrtle. Well, thanks anyway."

Myrtle went back home, still frowning. When she walked inside, Miles and Wanda were looking at her expectantly. Puddin leaped out of a kitchen chair, where she'd been drinking a Coke, and started resentfully wiping down the sink.

"How did it go?" asked Miles.

"I was going to write it off as a complete and total waste of time, but I have the feeling somehow that I *did* get some information. I'm just not entirely sure what it is that I got. Erma was full of nonsense, as usual, and her home was strewn with medical equipment. She said that I had the reputation of a bad cook, which was a bizarre thing to say," said Myrtle.

Miles and Wanda exchanged glances. Puddin made a snorting sound from the kitchen.

Myrtle said, "So she wasn't really making a lot of sense, but still there was something in there that was a kernel of information. It's just lost in all of Erma's ridiculousness."

"Maybe if you think about it for a while you'll realize what it was," said Miles.

"I suppose so. I think it's time to check in with Sloan about another special report on Preston's death. I'll run down to the newspaper office shortly."

Wanda said carefully, "I was gonna ask Miles if he could take me back home."

Myrtle's eyes widened. "Back home? Is something wrong with Crazy Dan?" Myrtle believed there were *many* things wrong with Crazy Dan, but it would be worse if there was now something extra-wrong with him.

Wanda looked solemn. "I gotta look after him. He's my brother. He's no good by himself. Gets crazier than usual."

Miles cleared his throat. "While you were gone, Wanda called him."

Myrtle raised her eyebrows. "The phone was connected over there still?"

Wanda nodded. "He paid the bills. The power's back on now. Said he ain't buyin' no more stuff fer a long time. He misses my cookin' and cleanin' and my company."

"Well, that *is* good news," said Myrtle, beaming. "But you know you're more than welcome to stay here. It's been a nice break for me."

Wanda looked a little sad. "Nice fer me, too. But I gotta take care of him."

Myrtle said, "You're a very responsible sister. I'll let you know what happens on *Tomorrow's Promise* since I know you don't have TV up there."

Puddin made a gasping sound from the kitchen at the thought of anyone not having a TV.

Wanda grinned mischievously. "Already know what's gonna happen."

Myrtle sighed. "I swear that I'll never understand how your gifts work. You can know future episodes of the soap opera, but don't know who our neighborhood murderer is."

Wanda shrugged. "That's just the way the sight works." She gave Myrtle a stern look. "Yer in danger."

Myrtle threw up her hands. "Yes, yes. But it seems like that's something I can't really avoid. You don't have any sense of when this mysterious danger is going to crop up, do you?"

Wanda shook her head sadly. "But it's right around the corner."

"I'll keep my eyes peeled," said Myrtle.

Myrtle set off while Wanda packed her few belongings so that Miles could take her back to the hubcap-covered shack. Puddin finally started noisily vacuuming.

Pasha slipped out of the door when Myrtle left and padded down the street until she caught up with her, being careful not to be seen.

A few minutes later, Myrtle opened the door to the dimly-lit newspaper office and squinted as her eyes adjusted to the lack of light. Pasha darted in behind her and stood sentry by the door. "Sloan?" Myrtle called out peremptorily in her best schoolteacher voice.

But there was no reply.

Myrtle sighed. She suspected Sloan's work ethic wasn't all it could be. He appeared to spend a good deal of time at the bar down the street. When asked about it, he always said that he was just gathering information for the paper from his informants. It sounded better than drinking beer and playing pool, she supposed.

She sat down at Sloan's desk to wait, fishing her phone out of her purse to give him a call and see when he intended to be back on the job.

The door swung open and Myrtle rose. "Sloan!" she said crossly.

But it was just Jenny Rollins.

"If you're looking for Sloan, he's out of the office," said Myrtle.

Jenny walked up to Myrtle. "Do you have any idea when he'll be back? I was going to give him the information on the craft marketplace the church is hosting."

"No idea," said Myrtle, still feeling grouchy over the whole thing. "He's abandoned his post. I'll give him a call to find out. He's probably down the street at the bar—I just don't feel like searching him out right now."

Myrtle plopped back down in Sloan's chair and Jenny sat in a chair next to her.

"How are you doing?" asked Myrtle, thinking about Puddin's proclamations about Jenny's grieving.

Jenny sighed. "Well, each day is something of a struggle, but one gets through it. I hear that it will get easier over time. You lost your husband, I know. How long did it take for you to resume life as normal?"

Myrtle considered this. "You know, it was so long ago that I don't even remember. Red was still a boy. At the time, I was so intent on making money to support the two of us and working out the will and the bills that I didn't even take time to grieve. Which is not what you're supposed to do." She paused. "And then, of course, I think the *way* one loses a husband can also contribute to grief."

Jenny winced. "You mean it's harder on you when someone shoves your husband down a staircase? I have to agree."

Myrtle froze. But she tried to keep her face calm and her voice level. "I'm sure it is, dear. Now, how about if I make that call to Sloan? He's clearly dilly-dallying somewhere—probably the local watering hole. I can get him here pronto."

Jenny tilted her head to one side and looked thoughtfully at Myrtle. "You know, Miss Myrtle, you had a funny expression on your face just a moment ago."

Myrtle gave a short laugh. "Oh, it's probably the barbeque talking back to me. I do enjoy barbeque, but sometimes it will chirp up for days."

Jenny's face was brooding. "Scotty mentioned you came by the restaurant. Then he said one of his coworkers was teasing him later about an older lady calling up and asking about his shifts. She thought it was cute. But when Scotty told me about it, I knew what it must mean."

Myrtle lifted her chin a little. Apparently, the jig was up. "You realized it must mean that Scotty's alibi was no good."

"Who was it who saw him leave the restaurant early?" asked Jenny in a carefully careless voice.

"A good reporter never names her sources," said Myrtle with a sniff. She punched a few numbers into her phone until Jenny swiftly knocked it away with a clatter onto the floor.

# Chapter Twenty-Two

"Sorry," she said. She really did look regretful. "I can't let you make that call, Miss Myrtle. It really wouldn't do to have a tipsy Sloan wander back in here right now."

Myrtle pushed the rolling chair back a bit to gain a little distance from Jenny. "So, let's see. We have a few pieces of information that are very interesting, don't we? First off, there's something that a good friend of mine mentioned a while ago. She spoke about the rain."

Jenny lifted a perfectly-groomed eyebrow. "She's a weather forecaster?" Jenny rummaged in her purse.

"No, she's a psychic. You met Wanda. You'd never guess it, but getting these little psychic insights are sort of like a shaky picture on a television full of static. She knows they're important, but she doesn't really know how they fit in. I didn't either, until just a few moments ago." Myrtle hoped that, by stalling, Sloan might realize he really did have a paper to publish before the end of the day. Surely he'd be walking in the door momentarily.

Jenny looked curious. "How does rain figure into the equation?"

"Cindy Cook said that Preston came home sopping wet. But Preston said that he'd left the garage and gotten home before the rainstorm hit. Why else would he lie about his movements?"

Jenny gave a small shrug and very gently removed a large wrench from her purse. "I'm guessing you've reached the conclusion that Preston killed my husband."

Myrtle saw the swish of a black tail behind Jenny and blinked. Then she quickly said, "I can't come to any other conclusion. I believe that Preston was upset with Royce for having an affair with his wife. He left the garage and headed over to town hall. Royce had shaken a lot of hands and had stayed a bit later. He also prided himself on taking the stairs instead of the elevator. I'm going to presume that the custodian, when locking up, used the elevator instead and that's why no one discovered Royce's body until I showed up the next morning."

Jenny's eyes had the thinnest veneer of tears covering them before she briskly batted her lashes a few times to rid herself of them. "I suppose so."

Myrtle took a deep breath. "The problem, Jenny, is that no one else knew how Royce died. Red expressly asked me not to say anything and I know he didn't say a word. But somehow you knew exactly how Royce was murdered."

"That's why your expression changed a minute ago," said Jenny dryly. "I knew a light bulb had gone off in your head."

"I've also been thinking a good deal about love," said Myrtle. "Do you watch *Tomorrow's Promise*?"

Jenny shook her head.

"Well lately, it's all been focused on different types of love. Naturally, the show being a soap opera, the love all turns out remarkably badly. It made me think of you, actually," said Myrtle. She saw Pasha's face. The black cat's eyes were narrowed as she peered, unseen, at Jenny.

Jenny was too elegant to snort, but she made an approximation of the sound. "Of me?"

"Yes. You seem this sort of tragic figure to me."

Jenny clearly didn't like this one bit. She straightened up in her chair, her hand gripping the wrench. "How do you figure that?"

"Here's how I see it. You're interrupting a love triangle, aren't you? You were the one who didn't belong. Cindy, Preston, Royce—they all went to high school together. They all have this history, this back-story. You're not from Bradley at all and just didn't have any context to their love story. You were the fourth wheel, so to speak."

Jenny didn't say anything, but her eyes watched Myrtle intently.

Myrtle took another deep breath and wondered why on earth Sloan was taking so long.

"My housekeeper told me you cared very deeply for Royce, although you present this very composed front to the world. Perhaps you were more devoted to Royce than he was to you. I understand something might have been amiss between the two of you because you slept in different rooms."

Jenny didn't seem at all surprised that Myrtle knew this rather personal bit of information. "Royce snored," she murmured.

"So what I believe happened is that you realized Preston had killed Royce. I think you *did* go to the town hall the night of the debate. You got there after the debate had ended and when the storm had started up. Royce liked to walk to town hall, you said. I think you didn't want him walking back in the rain—or maybe he called and asked you to come pick him up. At any rate, you drove over there. When you arrived, you saw Preston leaving . . . and probably Erma Sherman arriving, as well. But Royce was nowhere to be seen. You hopped out of the car and found him."

Jenny slumped just a little in her seat at the memory.

Myrtle said, "But there was nothing you could do. Royce was beyond help. And here you were, Royce's wife, and at the scene of a crime. You'd know, of course, that spouses are always the prime suspect in a murder case. You went back home and figured no one would be the wiser."

"Except for you," said Jenny dryly.

"Well, naturally. So you knew the truth about Royce's death and you were heartbroken. You decided to enact revenge on Preston for killing your husband." Myrtle paused. "Erma was extremely loud at Royce's funeral, saying that she'd seen something important. Preston, who'd seen headlights when he was leaving the town hall, likely thought Erma had seen *him*. He left the garage late the other night and headed out to take care of Erma so that she wouldn't expose him as the murderer. What he didn't know is that you had been carrying out surveillance on him, looking for just the right opportunity to enact your revenge."

Jenny smiled a little condescendingly. "You really think I was sneaking around in your neighbor's yard to kill Preston Cook?"

"Yes, I really do. I don't think, as a rule, it's something you'd *ordinarily* do, Jenny. But your emotions got the better of you. I think your desperation is evident right now, too, and that's why you're here. Why wouldn't you have just emailed the information to Sloan about the church event? Why would that even be something the church would put you in charge of right now *anyway*, with your husband just-buried? No, you followed me here, the same way you followed Preston. It has to do with another type of love, doesn't it?"

Jenny tilted her head to one side. "You've lost me."

"A mother's love. My questions to Scotty are starting to make him wonder exactly where you were when Preston was murdered. He's covered for you because he knows you weren't at home like he says you were. The only problem is that now his own alibi is falling apart because he wasn't working as late as he says he was. You're worried, as his mom, that he's going to become more of a suspect. So you're here to silence me. Just the way you silenced Preston." Myrtle glanced at the heavy wrench. "You're fond of blunt force trauma it would seem."

Jenny opened her mouth to respond, but never did. At that moment, Pasha decided to leap on Sloan's desk, right in front of Jenny. What's more, Pasha hissed, her lips drawn back over a sparkling array of sharp teeth.

Jenny gave a short shriek and pushed back away from the desk. Myrtle took the opportunity to head quickly for the door.

Unfortunately, Jenny was much younger and it took her mere seconds to recover from the shock of seeing a very angry black cat unexpectedly in front of her. Plus, Myrtle, usually fairly surefooted, stumbled over a pile of clutter in the dimly-lit newsroom.

Apparently, according to the shriek Myrtle heard behind her, Pasha must have taken the opportunity to leap somewhere on Jenny with all of her claws poking into her. Then the cat yowled angrily as Jenny apparently flung her off.

Jenny grabbed Myrtle from behind and shoved her on the floor, raising the wrench.

Suddenly, the newsroom was flooded with light and Sloan stood there, looking thunderstruck at the sight of local socialite Jenny preparing to hit his old schoolteacher on the head with a wrench. "Jenny?" he asked slowly.

"Call Red," said Myrtle in her most commanding voice and Sloan immediately dug his phone out of his pocket. To Jenny, she said in a steely tone, "Put the wrench down."

Jenny didn't, but was so distracted by the sight of Sloan dialing Red that Myrtle was able to knock it out of her hand with her cane.

Jenny took off for the door, pushing the still-shocked Sloan out of the way.

Myrtle rushed after her, yelling, "Stop! Murderer! Help!"

Jenny came to a skidding stop right outside the newspaper office. Wanda and Miles were standing there, Wanda staring gravely at Jenny.

"Where you gonna go?" asked Wanda intently. "Gonna leave yer boy?"

Jenny's shoulders slumped. Then she slowly shook her head.

Wanda said, "Should'a slept. Shouldn't have gone out that night and done what you did."

## MURDER ON THE BALLOT

Jenny nodded and quietly said, "I know."

After that, Jenny was quite placid as they waited a few minutes for Red to appear. Jenny stood demurely with her hands folded and a blank expression on her face. Wanda stood silent and grim. Miles looked nervously around, hoping Red would appear at any moment. Pasha gave herself a bath and then loped away. Myrtle convinced Sloan that she must be the one to write the story and that perhaps it qualified as a rare "special edition" for the newspaper. Onlookers craned their necks curiously as they strolled by.

Red finally arrived, looking hassled. Lieutenant Perkins was right behind him. "Mama," he groaned.

Myrtle threw up her hands. "I didn't do a single thing, Red! Jenny *stalked* me. She followed me into the newsroom and created the entire scene."

"So I need to add 'stalker' to the list of crimes I hear Jenny has committed?" Red looked at Jenny and said, "I have to admit I'm surprised by this, Jenny. I never had you down as a murderer."

Myrtle said, "That's how she was able to fly under the radar."

Perkins smiled at Myrtle. "Sort of the way *you're* able to fly under the radar, I suppose."

Myrtle beamed at him as if he were a favorite student. "Precisely! Everyone tends to underestimate the elderly, don't they?"

"To their detriment, if they're dealing with you," muttered Red. He turned to Jenny. "Now, what have we got on our hands here? Two murders?"

A flash of dislike appeared on Jenny's features. "Just the one."

"She'd never have done anything to hurt Royce," said Myrtle. "That's the whole point."

"Should'a just slept," murmured Wanda again.

Red gave Wanda an apprehensive look. Then he glanced around him where a small crowd of onlookers was gaping at them. "All right, first things first. Let's move this conversation off the sidewalk and into the station."

"Everyone?" asked Miles, looking uneasily around him. He apparently did not want to be in this parade of killers and witnesses heading to the police station.

"Everyone," said Red firmly as he handcuffed Jenny and strode with her down the street to the small police station at the town hall.

It was quite a motley crew parading down the sidewalk. Miles looked down at the sidewalk as Myrtle puffed up with pride and was practically waving as they went.

"Miles," she hissed at him. "You look very guilty with your head down like that. Everyone's going to think that you're the culprit or had something to do with it."

Miles said darkly, "I had nothing to do with any of it. I hardly think anyone is going to believe otherwise, considering that Jenny is the one in handcuffs."

They quickly arrived at the station. Perkins set up a digital recorder to record everyone's statements while Red took the more old-fashioned approach of finding actual paper statements for everyone to fill out. Miles jotted down what he'd seen when he'd arrived at the station. Wanda dictated her account. Sloan, who was now getting a bit sleepy from the effects of his midday beer drinking, quickly wrote down what had happened when he'd opened the newsroom door and then asked to be excused.

"Good idea," drawled Red. "In fact, I'm going to go ahead and ask Wanda and Miles to leave too, since we have their accounts, if that's okay with Lt. Perkins." Perkins gave a nod and Red continued, "This police station is too small. Mama, I do want to hear a little more of an explanation as to what happened from you. And Jenny—well, you know you're detained for the foreseeable future."

Myrtle said, "I do have one question for Wanda before she goes. How did you end up at the newspaper office? Miles was taking you back home."

Wanda said in a quiet voice, "You was in danger."

Myrtle felt very relieved The Sight had finally provided a little clarity in its message.

After the others left, Red prompted his mother. "Now. Let me hear how you ended up in this situation."

Myrtle put her nose in the air. "I was simply minding my own business."

Perkins smiled at her. "What makes me think that you might have also wanted to speak with the editor about writing a story about Preston's murder?"

Myrtle gave him an admiring look. "You're absolutely right. In fact, now Sloan has assigned me with an even bigger story. This one. Anyway, as I said, I was minding my own business."

Jenny made a disbelieving huffing noise.

Perkins said to her, "You disagree with that, Mrs. Rollins?"

Jenny said, "I certainly do. The last thing Myrtle Clover does is to mind her own business. She minds *everyone else's* business. That's why we're all here right now."

Myrtle gave her a cold look. "No, the reason we're all here right now is because you took the ill-advised approach of taking justice into your own hands."

Jenny opened her mouth to respond and then shut it again.

Myrtle said, "That's right. You don't have a response to that because it's true. Instead of informing the police that you'd seen Preston leaving a crime scene, you decided to mete out your own justice in the form of revenge."

Jenny's eyes narrowed. "I already told you—"

"Oh, I'm well-aware of what you've already told me. You didn't want to call the police because you thought it would make *you* look guilty because *you'd* been at a crime scene. I'm sorry, but that just doesn't wash with me. What happened is that you were furious. Even though you knew Royce wasn't faithful to you, you still loved him fiercely. I heard accounts of how protective you were towards him in public if you felt he was being attacked in any way. You were angry you couldn't provide that role of protector in time to save him . . . so you switched it, didn't you? You set out to enact revenge on his killer."

Jenny had already been informed of her rights, of course, however she seemed inclined to forget the need of an attorney as Myrtle got her riled up. Perhaps Jenny Rollins had never been challenged in such a way. At any rate, it made her see red.

"Why shouldn't I have?" she said in a haughty tone. "I had no guarantee that he was going to be apprehended for killing my husband. And no guarantee that a jury of his peers wouldn't be stupid enough to give him a minor sentence."

"So you stalked Preston," said Myrtle.

"*Followed* him," corrected Jenny, shortly.

Myrtle narrowed her eyes. "If you were waiting outside his home, you were stalking him, not following him."

Red groaned. "Mama, can we dispense with the semantics right now and get on with it?"

"Fine! So you saw Preston leave the garage very late and head home. Then you saw him head toward Erma Sherman's house," said Myrtle.

Jenny just watched her with cold eyes.

Myrtle continued, "You must not have been too surprised, however. After all, Erma had made quite a scene at Royce's funeral reception, claiming to have information that she was going to pass on to Red about Royce's death. That was clearly why you decided to stake out his house. Preston must have been sweating bullets, worried sick about being exposed."

"He was a ridiculous man," snapped Jenny. "He tried to talk to me at Royce's *funeral*, blaming Royce for having an affair with Cindy. No respect for me or for the dead. I didn't want to hear anything about it."

"He was *so* ridiculous, in fact, that you decided to murder him. So you did—right there in Erma's yard. Erma, who's become something of a light sleeper, heard some noise out there. You slipped away before she could investigate and drove back home where you could plead ignorance to the murder. But there was someone who knew you weren't where you'd said—Scotty."

Jenny looked down at the linoleum floor of the police station.

Myrtle said, "Scotty, being a loyal son, wasn't quite sure what you'd been doing, but knew you needed an alibi. So he gave you one. The only problem is that Scotty wasn't actually working when he said he was that night. It made it look like *Scotty* was the one who'd killed Preston, even though he'd only given the wrong information to protect you."

"You were determined to find out that Scotty had lied about when he'd worked," said Jenny.

Red chuckled. "Mama has a way of getting into other people's business, Jenny. I know you're not from around here, but that's something everybody knows here in Bradley."

Perkins said, "So what made you decide to come after Mrs. Clover?"

"*Stalk* me," said Myrtle.

Jenny said, "No, no. I actually *followed* this time. I didn't wait outside your house, I just happened to see you as I was walking through downtown. I thought it might be a good time to find out exactly how much you knew—and if you were suspecting Scotty."

Myrtle snorted inelegantly. "I think there was a little more thought to it than that and a lot more malice. I hardly believe that Jenny carries a heavy wrench around with her on a daily basis."

Jenny shrugged.

Myrtle said, "The problem was that Jenny didn't think before she spoke. So she ended up telling me that Royce was pushed down a staircase."

Red's and Perkins's eyebrows shot up simultaneously.

"That's right," said Myrtle smugly. "Jenny knew precisely how her husband had died, even though Red said that information was to be kept secret. After that, everything devolved into a total circus."

"If Jenny immediately pulled out the wrench, how did you manage to get away from her?" asked Perkins with interest.

"Pasha. My little love."

Jenny made an irritated click with her tongue.

Perkins frowned and Red explained, "Mama's feral friend. It's a black cat."

"And she's brilliant."

Red gave Myrtle a doubtful look, but didn't seem to want to argue the point.

"Pasha defended me with great passion and earnestness, surprising Jenny enough so I could run toward the door. But Sloan's clutter derailed me and I tripped over one of the many boxes he left scattered all over the floor. He fortunately redeemed himself by returning from the bar or wherever he was and interrupting Jenny before she could silence me, too," said Myrtle.

Jenny pressed her lips together.

"Okay, well, I've heard enough," said Perkins. "We're going to need to get you processed, Mrs. Rollins. Mrs. Clover, I hope you're going to go home and put your feet up for a while."

"Oh, I will. As I write the news story about how I solved the case," said Myrtle, with a sly look at Red.

Red growled.

"Or I could re-open my bid for town council," said Myrtle with a sweet smile.

"Happy reporting," said Red dryly.

# About the Author:

Elizabeth writes the Southern Quilting mysteries and Memphis Barbeque mysteries for Penguin Random House and the Myrtle Clover series for Midnight Ink and independently. She blogs at ElizabethSpannCraig.com/blog, named by Writer's Digest as one of the 101 Best Websites for Writers. Elizabeth makes her home in Matthews, North Carolina, with her husband. She's the mother of two.

Sign up for Elizabeth's free newsletter to stay updated on releases:

https://bit.ly/2xZUXqO

# This and That

I love hearing from my readers. You can find me on Facebook as Elizabeth Spann Craig Author, on Twitter as elizabethscraig, on my website at elizabethspanncraig.com, and by email at elizabethspanncraig@gmail.com.

A special thanks to John DeMeo and Karen Young for their support!

Thanks so much for reading my book...I appreciate it. If you enjoyed the story, would you please leave a short review on the site where you purchased it? Just a few words would be great. Not only do I feel encouraged reading them, but they also help other readers discover my books. Thank you!

Did you know my books are available in print and ebook formats? Most of the Myrtle Clover series is available in audio and some of the Southern Quilting mysteries are. Find the audiobooks here.

Please follow me on BookBub for my reading recommendations and release notifications.

I have Myrtle Clover tote bags, charms, magnets, and other goodies at my Café Press shop: https://www.cafepress.com/cozymystery

If you'd like an autographed book for yourself or a friend, please visit my Etsy page.

I'd also like to thank some folks who helped me put this book together. Thanks to my cover designer, Karri Klawiter, for her awesome covers. Thanks to Freddy Moyano for the concept! Thanks to my editor, Judy Beatty for her help. Thanks to beta readers Amanda Arrieta and Dan Harris for all of their helpful suggestions and careful reading. Thanks to my ARC readers for helping to spread the word. Thanks, as always, to my family and readers.

# Other Works by Elizabeth:

M yrtle Clover Series in Order (be sure to look for the Myrtle series in audio, ebook, and print):

Pretty is as Pretty Dies
Progressive Dinner Deadly
A Dyeing Shame
A Body in the Backyard
Death at a Drop-In
A Body at Book Club
Death Pays a Visit
A Body at Bunco
Murder on Opening Night
Cruising for Murder
Cooking is Murder
A Body in the Trunk
Cleaning is Murder
Edit to Death
Hushed Up
A Body in the Attic
Murder on the Ballot
Death of a Suitor (2021)

**Southern Quilting Mysteries in Order:**
Quilt or Innocence
Knot What it Seams
Quilt Trip
Shear Trouble
Tying the Knot
Patch of Trouble
Fall to Pieces
Rest in Pieces
On Pins and Needles
Fit to be Tied
Embroidering the Truth
Knot a Clue
Quilt-Ridden (2021)

**The Village Library Mysteries in Order (Debuting 2019):**
Checked Out
Overdue
Borrowed Time
Hush-Hush
Where There's a Will (2021)

**Memphis Barbeque Mysteries in Order (Written as Riley Adams):**
Delicious and Suspicious
Finger Lickin' Dead
Hickory Smoked Homicide
Rubbed Out

**And a standalone "cozy zombie" novel:** Race to Refuge, written as Liz Craig

Made in United States
North Haven, CT
09 December 2022